"A translator arrives at a residency on the Dalmatian coast with plans to make headway on a new project when a case of confused identity dissolves the borders between art and life. Natalie Bakopoulos writes with such potent beauty about the liminality of travel, self-conception, and the way translation remakes a story into a different version of itself. *Archipelago* is a lyric and profound meditation on what can happen when our sense of self becomes, as the narrator puts it, 'productively unhinged.' This novel is a gorgeously sly page-turner."
—LAURA VAN DEN BERG,
author of *State of Paradise*

"*Archipelago* is a gorgeous, haunting novel about translation, narrative, and the slippage between selves: who we are and who others believe us to be. We follow our narrator-traveler on her dreamlike journey, from one achingly beautiful setting to another, from one memory to another, tantalized and unsettled by her every encounter. With this novel, Bakopoulos weaves a spell and a mystery and makes something wholly her own."
—LYDIA KIESLING,
author of *Mobility*

MORE PRAISE FOR
Natalie Bakopoulos

"The clarity of insight about love and loss and grief will break you and remake you."
—JESMYN WARD,
author of *Let Us Descend*

"Bakopoulos reveals how lives, families, and countries fall together and apart in this thing we call life."
—STACEY D'ERASMO,
author of *The Complicities*

"Bakopoulos writes of her expatriates and exiles, immigrants and refugees, with such intimacy, tenderness and wisdom, intuiting as she does that these are all states of grief. The stoicism with which her characters bear their various loses—portrayed in limpid, pensive prose reminiscent of Rachel Cusk—is deeply affecting."
—PETER HO DAVIES,
author of *A Lie Someone Told You About Yourself*

"Observed in the manner of Elena Ferrante and Rachel Cusk."
—CLAIRE VAYE WATKINS,
author of *I Love You but I've Chosen Darkness*

archipelago

ALSO BY NATALIE BAKOPOULOS

Scorpionfish

The Green Shore

archipelago

a novel

natalie bakopoulos

TIN HOUSE / PORTLAND, OREGON

This is a work of fiction. All of the characters, organizations, and events portrayed in this novel are either products of the author's imagination or are used fictitiously.

CREDITS: p.iv and 135: Eleni Vakalo, excerpts from "The Forest," from *Before Lyricism*, edited and translated from Greek by Karen Emmerich. Copyright © 2017, 2018 by the Estate of Eleni Vakalo. English translation copyright © 2017, 2018 by Karen Emmerich. Reprinted with permission. | p.iv: Rachel Carson, excerpt from *The Edge of the Sea*. Copyright © 1955 by Rachel L. Carson. Used by permission. | p.1: Etel Adnan, excerpt from *Shifting the Silence*. Copyright © 2020 by Etel Adnan. Reprinted with permission. | p.53: Anne Carson, excerpt from "Decreation: How Women Like Sappho, Marguerite Porete, and Simone Weil Tell God," from *Decreation: Poetry, Essays, Opera*. Copyright © 2005 by Anne Carson. Reprinted with permission. | p.155: Mary Ruefle, excerpt from "Pause," from *My Private Property*. Copyright © 2016 by Mary Ruefle. Reprinted with permission. | p.183: Olivia Laing, excerpt from *To the River*. Copyright © 2011 by Olivia Laing.

Copyright © 2025 by Natalie Bakopoulos

First US Edition 2025
Printed in the United States of America

All rights reserved. No part of this book may be used or reproduced in any manner whatsoever without written permission from the publisher except in the case of brief quotations embodied in critical articles or reviews. For information, contact Tin House, 2617 NW Thurman Street, Portland, OR 97210.

Manufacturing by Lake Book Manufacturing
Interior design by Beth Steidle

Library of Congress Cataloging-in-Publication Data

Names: Bakopoulos, Natalie, author.
Title: Archipelago : a novel / Natalie Bakopoulos.
Description: Portland, Oregon : Tin House, 2025.
Identifiers: LCCN 2025007757 | ISBN 9781963108309 (paperback) | ISBN 9781963108378 (ebook)
Subjects: LCGFT: Novels.
Classification: LCC PS3602.A5933 A88 2025 | DDC 813/.6—dc23/eng/20250310
LC record available at https://lccn.loc.gov/2025007757

Tin House
2617 NW Thurman Street, Portland, OR 97210
www.tinhouse.com

Distributed by W. W. Norton & Company

1 2 3 4 5 6 7 8 9 0

For Jeremy

And so in my mind's eye these coastal forms merge and blend in a shifting, kaleidoscopic pattern in which there is no finality, no ultimate and fixed reality—earth becoming fluid as the sea itself.

—RACHEL CARSON,
The Edge of the Sea

The shape of the forest has
The shape of a jellyfish
That you catch in your hands and it slips through
As a wave
Pushes it out

—ELENI VAKALO,
"The Forest," translated by Karen Emmerich

I

Etel Adnan writes: "My favorite time is in time's other side, its other identity, the kind that collapses and sometimes reappears, and sometimes doesn't."

I attribute all that summer's disquiet to an encounter with a man on the ferry, an encounter that was as destabilizing as it was strange.

I have always been charmed by ferry rides. Unlike many of the regulars who prefer to sit inside, used to the routine ride and its accompanying seascape, I usually spend the voyage on the top open deck, reading, drinking coffee, taking in the view. Sometimes you might glimpse a school of dolphins surfacing in the distance, or a flock of seagulls surrounding another boat, making it look as though the boat itself might take off and fly away.

Land looks corporeal when rising from the water, curving and sloping like figures reclining in the sun.

Bodies of land.

That May morning, though, the Aegean sky was hazy, and I couldn't see too much in the distance. Dust clouds from the Sahara had filtered much of Greece to a startling orange, and everything was covered in a blurry film.

Half an hour into the route, at the concession stand for a coffee, I ran into an acquaintance. She, a journalist, had boarded the ferry on the previous island, where her mother was born and still lived. I had not seen her in several years, but I had been following her work, which covered tourism and sustainability in the Aegean, particularly islands such as

Mykonos and Santorini, which received tens of thousands of visitors per day. These islands had long drawn huge numbers of tourists. But the new development everywhere, particularly these Western Cycladic islands we were sailing between, had unsettled her.

We walked back to the benches and found a seat. Places are becoming backdrop, she said.

I'd been coming from an island Lawrence Durrell had dismissed as having "not much to see." I'd been going there since I was a teenager, when my aunt and uncle bought their small, charming house near the port. "Not much to see" was relative, of course. It was a quiet, relaxing island. Now, development had charged ahead at a frenetic pace, more quickly than the island's infrastructure could or should have to handle. The summer before, traffic had bottlenecked near certain popular beaches, and the island's main town, in the evenings, had crawled with bodies. Rental car places had proliferated, yet they still always seemed out of cars. Water shortages had become normal, and the stress of vehicles and delivery trucks and hotels was wreaking havoc on the land. A travel magazine had showcased its neighboring island, from where my friend had been coming, as "undiscovered," even though they both have long been beloved by Athenians, to say nothing of the locals for whom these islands were home.

My cousin Effie lived on that island with not much to see for part of the year with her two daughters. I often rented a small, inexpensive traditional studio nearby. That late spring she was still in Athens, and because I needed a new place to live, she had invited me to stay in her home. I'd opened it up for the season, running errands and helping her prepare for the first round of renters, before she and her family settled in later that summer.

The beach where we used to swim, I told my friend, once had a few random beach chairs placed there by locals for anyone to use. I laughed, telling her about an old four-poster bed that had spent an entire summer rooted in the sand, dragged down from someone's house. Sometimes you might find someone asleep there, snoring away.

My friend laughed too and said, I can picture it. Then she glanced around. Nearby, a group of teenagers huddled over someone's phone, watching something and laughing. Across the benches, an older woman dressed in widow's black, including black Adidas sneakers, wore a face mask below her chin, as was the fashion. She watched the teenagers with a mix of amusement and appraisal. On the benches next to us, a woman our age, about fifty, sat with her little dog, reading, her feet propped on the bench across from her.

My favorite place, I told my friend, had been a small, excellent taverna that once sat at the top of the beach, nestled beneath a fig tree, with live music on Sunday afternoons: rebetika, old Greek pop, songs that everyone knew. Several years ago, it had been sold and remodeled and was now a café that blared its loud, clubby music from open until close. The beach was covered with reclining chairs that cost fifty dollars to rent, a bargain compared to some of the more touristy islands nearby. Even if you drape your blanket in the sand, I said, the café owner comes around and asks for money.

My friend nodded in recognition and disgust.

But I still loved that beach. Each morning, I swam there and dried off in the sun until the music began to sound. When I ascended the path back up to the road, the young staff members, always a bit bleary eyed and pained with lack of sleep from the night before, waved at me. They sat at a corner table and drank their coffee and seemed to find the requisite music, which began promptly at nine o'clock, just as insufferable as I did.

And all this was for whom, exactly?

Even if I could afford it, my friend said, I wouldn't pay money to sit in a chair.

I nodded. Development was normal and inevitable, I knew, and hard to avoid. The shift may have been gradual but to me seemed to have happened all at once.

They should shut him down, my friend said. That's illegal. Shut the whole place down.

That's when I felt we were being watched. I glanced around. The ferry deck was not crowded. It was early in the season, and between the dust and the wind, most people chose to sit inside. My friend stood to take a call.

My mother, she said to me, when she hung up. She forgot I was just there.

I nodded.

My friend gathered her things. She was parked below, which always made her anxious, she said, so she wanted to wait at her car. I wished her a good summer.

Alone, I was seized by an uncanny déjà vu. As though I had had this conversation before, with a friend, right before she went to get her car. Faces felt strange, as if they were put together incorrectly, and I felt a chill move from my neck to my spine. I felt nauseated, like I was getting a migraine, wanted to shield my eyes from the hazy light. I moved to the bench across from me, so I could face the other direction.

There was the man, staring, his gaze somewhere between intimate and hostile. How long had he been right behind us, listening, watching? About my age, perhaps a bit older, dressed in nice jeans and suede sneakers, a waxed motorcycle jacket. A chiseled face, with neat, thick eyebrows. He kept touching his cheeks, as though his beard had suddenly disappeared and he'd not yet become accustomed to this smoothness.

I did not recognize him. I met his eyes a moment and hoped he'd understand that I was not who he thought. I was someone else.

When the group of teenagers jumped up from their bench and shuffled by, he dropped his eyes, shifting his gaze to follow them. Then he walked to the front of the ferry and leaned his elbows along the railing. I had the sense that his turning away was a provocative gesture meant to insult me.

At first I wondered if he had been involved with my friend, if his rage had been directed at her.

I glanced around. The woman with the little dog was no longer there, and the yiayia slept with the posture of a dancer, her hands folded on her lap. Someone had draped a pink hoodie over her shoulders. I could not help it, I turned to look over my shoulder and there he was, still standing against the railing but now looking toward me. Almost a glare.

Before I'd run into my friend, I'd been on the top deck alone, in the sun, reading Anita Brookner's *Look at Me*. (No, coincidental; I don't mean the man took it literally.) Brookner says we see a woman's melancholia as coming from her mind, whereas for a man it comes from suffering from romantic love. A melancholy woman is her *own* disease, she says, emphasis mine, whereas a man's melancholia, it might imply, is also her disease. This man on the ferry may have been tormented by romantic love: both torment's object and subject, stuck in its middle voice.

In fact, I had encountered this type of person quite often as a younger woman, until I came to understand the pattern. How many of us, at some point, have mistaken obsession for love? I was projecting, of course.

Because maybe our conversation had irritated him, a café owner, say, or a developer, someone pressuring the municipality to allow for more building, someone trying to get around protection laws, to privatize the coastline, which in Greece was public. A few months before, an ecologist had had all her car windows shattered in Athens, for her work preserving a stretch of coastal forest that developers had been eyeing for a resort. A month later, an archaeologist had been beaten outside his home; his work preserving cultural antiquities on Mykonos had blocked a new hotel. These were extremes, I knew. But things happened. And violence always arose from possession; the question was only when and where, and from whom.

The announcement on the ferry sounded to begin disembarking, and my thoughts shifted to the personal, to self-blame. I was certain I had known this man on the ferry, had even at some point in my life upset him. His anger toward me was palpable, and I felt fractured and somehow ashamed, the shame I had always felt when I had not given someone what they wanted, had shown myself not to be the person someone else had decided I was, to fit their own needs.

I left the top deck and waited in the crowd on the staircase. I couldn't get off the ferry quickly enough. I rushed off the gangway into the flow of bodies and cars.

I was headed to the airport and needed a taxi, so I veered away from the people streaming off the ferry and the impatient passengers ready to board. That was when I heard the rev of an engine and felt the accelerating speed of something behind me. I jumped out of the way and lost my balance, tripping to the ground as the car swerved past. He nearly ran over my suitcase. Our eyes met in his rearview mirror, and from what I could see, his expression was unmoving. Someone behind me shouted after him. My pulse raced yet I felt frozen.

I didn't think he was trying to hit me, but he wanted me to know he could have. I brushed myself off; my palms were scraped, and bits of gravel had stuck in my jeans. An older couple, a man and woman, stopped, the woman putting her hand on my shoulder and the man swearing after the driver. They asked if I was okay and I couldn't answer.

The crowd oozed down the gangway as if from a hose.

THE SMALL CAFÉ AT THE PORT HAD EMPTIED AS PEOPLE got ready to board. A few taxi drivers approached me but I fiddled with my phone, using an app to call one instead, not wanting something so unscripted. I did not feel like haggling over a price and somehow felt safer if my movements were tracked.

When the taxi arrived, I was reassured by the driver's large brown eyes and kind face. Without more than a word or two, he sped us off to the airport. I was grateful he was not the chatty type. I fussed with my bag, my phone, the bracelets on my wrist until I finally calmed down and stared out the window. Everything remained covered with that fine orange dust, the city filtered through a tangerine haze. On the bus ahead of us, someone had written in the orangey grime: TOURISTS GO HOME.

A particular image appeared in my mind, that of a narrow inlet of sand with water on both sides; this was a beach I sometimes went to on the island. It was called, I think, a tombolo, but since my first visit there as a teen, I'd called it the land river. What I liked best about it was the small dune hill that separated the sides. You could have your blanket laid out and have no idea who had set up their place on the other side of the slope. Once in a while, I'd peer over the dune and then settle back down on my blanket.

More than once, I'd spent an hour or more on that beach before finding my cousins, who were equally surprised to see me, standing up and looking across at me over the dune. This hiddenness, my knowledge of another complete beach scene happening over the sloped sandy pillow as I went about my swimming and sunning and reading, was comforting.

Everywhere in Greece, people were worrying, rightfully, about erosion: even the stress of all those cars, parking at the beaches, could have irrevocable implications. Yet the municipality had recently decided to level the natural dunes, destroying all the vegetation along with them, privileging the photographic over the ecologic. Somehow, the flatness of the landscape was found to be more appealing than any unruly growth. My cousin told me that now, it was quite common to see yachts anchored off both shores.

I have always said that Instagram reduces place to a genre, and that the word "picturesque" renders places invisible, but this blatant destruction of the landscape, which would make it far more vulnerable to further loss, was a new kind of grotesque retrograde, as upsetting to me as the cosmetic distortions we were expected to make to our faces, all in the name of denying the future, and of looking the same.

I always returned to this beach in my mind: when unable to fall asleep, when hit by a bout of anxiety; sometimes it appeared to me randomly. I imagined a film running forward and backward, the dune rising up and leveling, rising up and leveling, as if time were moving in two directions, as if it were this easy to reconstruct what had been razed.

When we arrived at the airport, the driver wished me a good trip and hoped that everything would be okay. I had barely spoken a word. I thanked him, on my way between countries that shared not a border but a sea, countries that seemed they might be easy to move between via ferry, but were not.

It seems appropriate I begin this story here, with a haze, a transposition, a dislocation, a movement between the borders of language and voice and home. Sand becomes the rocky shore, the rocky shore becomes sand.

Find a beginning.

THE FLIGHT FROM ATHENS TO SPLIT WAS DELAYED SEVERAL hours, for reasons of visibility. I felt I'd never leave the airport, that I would stay there forever. But of course I did leave, and soon after I began my stay at an international arts center in a residency program for translation on a Croatian island off the Dalmatian coast. The stay was two weeks, and I had no plans after that. For the first time in my adult life, I was completely untethered.

On the first night, I woke with a start, completely unaware of where I was: Was I in motion, or was I standing still? Out loud I said: I have no way of knowing.

I'm in a box, I thought. I even wrote it down: This is not a place but a box. I need to walk through the forest, I need to walk to the sea. I forced myself out of the bed, even though I felt pinned to it. I stumbled out to the balcony in my pajamas, where I could get a glimpse of the intimate Adriatic, lit up by the moon. Perspective is always a relief.

I made it out of my room and down into the shared kitchen, where I poured myself a glass of sparkling water, downed it, and poured another glass from the tap. I walked onto the shared terrace, which overlooked the sea. Two of the younger translators had returned from the bar and were eating pasta—the kitchen looked like they'd cooked for the whole center—laughing hysterically about something. Their joy calmed me down, and I suddenly felt sleepy and safe. I returned to my room and slept well until sunrise.

The next morning, the restlessness had disappeared. I drank a coffee on my balcony, which faced the small, curvy street, and balconies across from me. If you sat with your chair to the side, feet propped up on the iron balustrade, you could glimpse the sea. Everyone on that street went out to their balconies and turned their bodies sideways, as if to watch a film. I was happy to be here, beside the sea, where I always felt more calm, more like myself.

After my coffee I went out for a walk, even feeling the urge for a run. I have always been a swimmer but never a dedicated runner, though I went through various phases where I thought I'd try. I was never successful; I hated running the way I hated most of the obligations my younger version placed upon herself for no discernible reason. So I stopped. Once in a while, on the long, brisk walks I still took every morning, I regained the urge to break into a jog. It never lasted more than ten minutes, and then I'd walk again. I recalled a summer when I was fifteen, staying with my paternal grandparents at their house near the Ionian Sea, the house where my father had lived as a child. It was the first summer I'd traveled there alone, and I felt grown-up and independent. Then, not yet accustomed to the afternoon nap, I ran in the heat of the afternoons, causing women hanging laundry in the garden to shout after me, as though I were in danger. From the house, not far from the impressive medieval fortress that loomed over the town—the Castle of Giants—I trotted down the old streets, bypassed the main town by the train station, and ended up at the olive groves that ran along the sea. At the beach I'd swim, dry off, and walk back to the house just as my grandparents were waking from their rest.

Croatia's landscape reminded me of Greece, but more bright and intense in its colors and somehow, to me, more serene in its disposition. But its language was not far, relatively speaking, from Ukrainian, my mother's native tongue. They were not mutually intelligible, and as far as Slavic languages go, a linguist might in fact call them distant. I would never claim a profound knowledge, either of the culture or of the place. But from the first time I heard it, I'd felt its comforting familiarity. Serbo-Croatian had been the language spoken in the household of my childhood best friend, who lived a few doors down in our Detroit suburb. His family, who'd called themselves Yugoslavian, had treated me as another daughter, and his grandmother, who spoke no English, would chatter away to me on their back porch while I, somehow happily, did my friend's math homework. She taught me songs. I liked being there. How do you understand what she's talking about, my friend would wonder, and I'd shrug because I could not explain it. I often understood what was meant but not exactly what was said.

To be multilingual, for me, was always more about abundance than fracture, and from a young age I loved this abundance. She's one of ours, his grandmother would always tell him, and he would roll his eyes and answer her in English. Sometimes my grandmother, my mother's mother, would come to retrieve me for dinner, and the two women, even with no English, seemed to be able to talk for a very long time in their own languages, somehow understanding each other enough for it to be pleasurable. And when my Greek grandmother visited she joined them too, a beyond-language encounter that has continued to fascinate me.

So I had nothing like fluency in Croatian, but I did have a working use of it. In my mid-thirties, I'd spent a year in a smaller city on the Dalmatian coast with my then partner, teaching at an international school. The setting had felt familiar even though it was foreign; there had been no relatives to keep tabs on us or shame us for making mistakes in the language, so I'd made mistakes and learned enough to get by. In that way, we were nameless. Of course there are also obligations to a place when you are a guest, but I had not yet understood them.

The morning was gorgeous, sunny and warm, and I took a walk up to the Venetian fortress. The smell of lavender was everywhere, tangles of vines climbed walls, and the morning breeze and the view of red-tiled roofs, the sea, the small archipelago of those wooded isles in the distance was topography I recognized. A nearby island had been closed to outsiders for decades, and served as a Yugoslavian military base, and I'd heard about bunkers and secret passageways and sunken ships. That was all decades ago now, a history layered over with newer histories, close to the surface yet also unearthed.

I sat on a bench and drank from my water bottle.

Again I sensed someone looking at me. This time a bearded man in expensive running clothes, pacing a bit, maybe cooling down from a run. His look was not necessarily aggressive but it was challenging, as if he were purposely seeing through me, as if I were both there and not there at all. Not invisible, but translucent as a jellyfish. It was not the man from the ferry, how could it be, yet a familiar fear stirred in my gut. It was probably nothing, but I stood and left.

THE PREVIOUS SUMMER, AN AMERICAN WOMAN HAD DISAPpeared in the southern Peloponnesus, not far from Kalamata, about half an hour away from the town where my father grew up. Her friends had said she'd gone hiking around another Venetian castle—you will find them scattered throughout the Mediterranean; the Venetians were interested in ports for trade—and another said they thought she'd gone to the famous waterfalls. These unsettling things happened everywhere, always, but when it happens in a place you know well, of course it feels closer. The US media reports painted the place as bellicose and menacing, as if layers of violence plunged vertically into the landscape and a woman hiking alone was bound to be a victim the moment she laced her shoes.

As if landscape created violence as opposed to being marked by it. Besides, humans create landscapes in the first place, border them, place them in a frame.

That summer she disappeared, fires had also ravaged the terrain, and in my mind these events remain linked. More than 150 fires in one week.

I suspected arson. Once the land burns, it's considered clear. So you can build on it.

When I was in college, my father's parents still had a small olive grove on beautiful land that ran along the sea, and after my run I'd wander through the trees, always finding them to be mysterious and knowing. After my grandparents died, my cousins sold the land. A few years later, much of the land in that area was damaged in a summer wildfire, and not long after, a hotel resort appeared. Olive trees are resilient, but I don't know if they have since recovered.

Anyway. Another American I'd met at a party in Athens, surprised that I traveled so much alone, asked me if I felt safe there. What she had meant by "there" was unclear. Europe? The Greek countryside? The Peloponnesus in particular? Athens? Even though for many years, until I'd decided to leave the States for good, I'd taught at a university in one of the quote unquote most dangerous cities in America, in a nation where daily mass shootings had become normalized, not to mention police brutality, in a nation that worshipped guns, in a nation where I'd been born and raised, in a nation where violence was inextricable from history.

There were places in Greece that had a sense of lawlessness about them, it's true, or a general sense of mystery, and there were a few times when driving at night along a bend, or on long ferry rides, where ships' lights lit up the foamy midnight sea, that I'd be overcome with a sudden fear. An inexplicable sense of foreboding, the feeling that the sea might swallow me up or that my car would go flying off a ledge, guided by something out of my control.

When I returned from my walk, some of the translators were on the terrace, drinking coffee and squinting at the sea, not saying a word. They waved at me and I smiled back. I spent the rest of the morning working in my room.

I HAD A GENEROUS DEADLINE, AND FOR THE FIRST TIME IN my life I felt I could work slowly, which felt nice because I had been rushing through life. My goal was to translate ten pages per day, half the speed of most other translators, but at the end of those two weeks I would have reached the book's halfway point.

My process this time was new. First, I had agreed to the project before reading it, which I had never done before. I was friendly with the writer, and the book had won several prizes already, both in Greece and in Europe. I had planned to read it through once, first, before I began, as I normally did. But even only a few lines in, I felt compelled to begin. I found myself translating as I went along, as though I wanted to live inside it and have it unfold before me through my translation of it. I wanted to try translating something as I was coming to know it, to understand it. To allow it to appear to me, through me. To tell a story before I knew its ending, the way stories are received, not told. Language, then something, then language.

A translation, for me, always begins at a metaphorical midnight, and at the midpoint, a shadowless noon, I feel I begin to understand something. A dream logic as sound and sensual as math. This time, not knowing how the story would unfold, I began doubly in the dark.

THAT FIRST FRIDAY, THE OTHER TRANSLATORS AND I TOOK the afternoon off and went for a boozy lunch. When the waiter brought us sweets, beautiful little cakes that looked like peaches, I felt happy and sleepy and calm from the meal, the rakija, the beer. The rest of the group wanted to check out a local artist's work in a gallery. I said I'd meet up with them later.

We were going to a play that evening, part of the cultural festival being sponsored by the institute that had invited us for this international translators' residency. I thought of the cool white sheets on that hard bed in my large but simple room, the big wooden table where I'd spread all my papers, my books, my laptop. A spare space, with wonderful light—I was happiest in these sorts of spaces, where I could work with very few traces of myself. The way the breeze filtered in, the wooden shutters, the surprisingly spacious balcony. My eyelids grew pleasantly heavy.

Once I began to walk in that late afternoon sun, though, I felt restless, not really wanting to go back to my room. The streets were quiet, even by the water, all the shops closed for the afternoon. A bookshop, the sort of eclectic island bookshop where you might find a cadre of expats living upstairs, a transient bunch of employees, was open—the famous one was of course in Paris; there was also one in Santorini, which I loved to visit when I was there. There was a hotel nearby like this, in fact, where travelers worked the front desk and housekeeping service in exchange for a room; the younger translators often hung out there because one of them had fallen in love with one of the travelers, and they drank beers late into the night together, on their rooftop.

The bookstore's front tables were full of books by writers who were guests at the festival, and I perused the ones in English. One translated from Polish, another from Danish; one by a Nigerian writer, and a debut novel by an American who I realized was also one of the translators, working from Bosnian. The fifth was by the British writer whom I had once spotted in my family's Greek hometown, where my father was born; she was rumored to have recently bought a house there. The town was an unlikely choice and she'd piqued local interest not necessarily because she was a writer, but because she was a foreigner who took an interest in the place, chatting with waitstaff and shop owners and the family who owned the antique furniture store. Maybe it would show up in one of her books.

Land and homes there were still relatively inexpensive, and I suppose there was an intrigue that came from not being one of the more chic and sought-after islands or even a town like Kardamyli, south of there, where Paddy Leigh Fermor had lived. Westerners writing about Greece have always held a particular spot in the Western literary imagination, nearly a genre of its own. Greece could remain a stranger, mysterious and ancient, but I could never see it that way.

I was surprised to see her among these other writers; she had a reputation for keeping to herself.

I had never met her before but over the years I seemed to catch glimpses of her, our lives in peculiar confluence, convergences probably only apparent to me. Like the time at a rooftop pool bar in a hotel in Athens, when I'd seen her chatting with the bartender. She had not yet reached the status she had now, but I'd loved her work from the beginning: the incisive, often eviscerating criticism; the enigmatic novels, the astute essays that made me feel like I had been recognized. I swam a few laps, the only one in the pool. Somewhat self-consciously, but except for the writer at the bar and another woman at the far end, talking on the phone, there was no one else up there.

Then this: Years later I read in one of her books a scene about a woman watching another swim laps in an Athens hotel pool and I felt the bizarre sensation of seeing a story from another point of view, a shift in camera perspective. Like when you see yourself in the background of someone else's photo, one you didn't realize was being snapped.

This is all speculation, of course. It could have been anyone. But I was sure it had been me.

Nobody was in the bookstore—whoever was working there seemed to have left for a break, leaving the store wide open—so I put the books down and left. I'd return later. At a small take-out coffee stand at the top of a hill I ordered a coffee and drank it quickly, which perked me up. As I descended the stairs, I thought of rejoining my friends at the gallery, and I stopped a moment, trying to decide.

From where I stood, I was nearly eye level with a rooftop terrace. A cocktail party, maybe a wedding. A few people stood at its edge, holding drinks, looking down at the street, and two men noticed me there. I was alone on this staircase, the little shops around it also closed, and I could feel their eyes remain on me.

Natalia, one of them called. And then once again, louder, clearer: Natalia.

NATALIA WAS NOT MY NAME—NOT EVEN CLOSE—BUT I looked up anyway and was surprised to recognize him: Luka, a writer I'd known for years. But when had I last seen him? I could not remember.

We'd met nearly twenty years before, during those early financial crisis years, when we were both in Athens. I was there on a fellowship and he had been working as a journalist. We often met for coffee. I loved his observations of Athens, his first time in the city. He was a journalist and a novelist and good at both, and he had the ability to arrive in a new place and read it. When I was back in the States and he in Berlin, he'd call me with completely random questions, which I figured were related to his writing. Quick: If you had a sailboat, what would you name it? Seasick, I'd say. (Luka did not have a boat nor did he have the money for one, so I imagined this was for a novel.) The questions had a playfulness to them, as though I were expected to answer without a second thought. Would you paint your kitchen yellow or green? Blue, I'd say. And so on.

Once in a while he'd call late at night, generally because of romantic distress: his first divorce; another tumultuous relationship; an unrequited love. But if I didn't have the time stamp as a marker of his mood, I could tell from the tone of his voice, the slower pace of his words, the way each conversation seemed to begin in medias res, as if I'd stumbled upon the recitation of some ancient oral epic. I could have been an invoked listener in a novel, a recipient of a letter. But if this sounds self-centered or narcissistic on his part, it wasn't, not quite. He was a kind man, overall, deeply generous in other ways, but it seemed when he talked to me he had the urge to self-narrate. I don't remember saying much during those conversations at all, but I remember them fondly.

But for no particular reason, we'd lost touch over the past few years. Because I knew Luka had grown up on the Dalmatian coast, where I'd heard he was now living, he'd been in the back of my mind when I arrived. In fact, this might be why I hadn't bothered calling him. Our paths always managed to cross.

So I said, Hi, Luka. I let him look at me a moment, realize and correct his mistake.

Come up, he said. I was wondering if you were here.

I didn't ask what the event was that I may have been crashing. Because of the arts festival, there were receptions and events everywhere. The night before I'd gone with a few others to a performance of various folk music from throughout the region, Croatian and Bosnian and Bulgarian, Macedonian, Greek, Turkish, and so on. The polyphonic singing of one group had been so stirring that I cried through their performance, then bought a CD, even though I had no way to play it. The songs reached so deep inside that I felt eviscerated. The music felt so familiar, as if it somehow encompassed all sides of me: my languages and my regrets and the griefs that piled up inside me, like stones.

Come up, Luka said again. The other man standing with him smiled, and I could feel their gazes as I ascended the staircase and rounded the corner, gesturing to the burly host that I was heading to the party. I did not know then, of course, that going up this winding staircase would be like walking through a one-way door.

THE OUTDOOR STAIRCASE TO THE ROOF, FROM WHERE Luka and the other man had stood and called to me, also wound around and around and around, and at the top I felt dizzy. I stood for a moment to gain my bearings. It had been sunny all day, an early summer warmth, but on my walk a bank of clouds had passed over. I wondered if it would rain. Yet in the short duration between my standing on the steps and walking out onto the terrace, the sun had returned. The hills in the distance glowed orange and pink.

The terrace was strewn with small cocktail tables, two seating areas with big outdoor couches, bars on both ends. I stopped and used the bathroom, smoothed my hair, which had become tangled and knotted, thick with salt. In the mirror I noticed something odd. I'd had, for months, a very small white bump on my lash line, something I'd meant to get removed but had hoped would go away on its own. The thought of an ophthalmologist removing it made me queasy. I knew it had been there that morning because in the harsh light of my bathroom I had re-noticed it, the way a new surrounding allows you to see your gray hairs, your aging skin, the stubborn weight around your waist. That small white bump was gone and a lone, loose eyelash sat atop my cheek. I forgot to make a wish and splashed cold water on my face, ran my wet hands through my hair, and applied lip balm. I'd been swimming the past afternoons and my skin seemed far more golden, my face more relaxed, than when I'd arrived.

I could see Luka at the terrace's far end, the same place where he'd called down to me—or to Natalia. He was broad shouldered, as I remembered, his hair honey brown. People were always flirting with him. He was a warm person, attentive but never solicitous; it was unlike him to make this sort of error and I was sure he would immediately correct himself.

Luka saw me as I was approaching the bar—I'd hoped to first get a drink—and waved me over. He and his friend were both smiling, and I assumed he'd realized his mistake.

I figured that before he had a chance to introduce me, I would introduce myself, but he was not the sort of person who forgot to introduce you, and there he was again: Natalia, he said, and the man offered his own name. Ivan, he said.

We worked on a translation together, Luka added. His dark eyes were friendly behind his thick-framed glasses.

This part was true, and I relaxed a bit. We'd co-translated a short excerpt of his work at a literary festival in Sofia. For this particular project, knowing the source language was not necessary; it had been an experiment in collaboration, in what translation really was. Though we'd been paired together randomly, we'd already known each other, and I remembered the experience as a fun one.

So though it was a strange way to identify me, he at least correctly remembered some context. That is, I both was and was not someone else. And I enjoyed this, felt a spark of prior familiarity or maybe simply potentiality, which might be why I was not insisting on correcting him. Besides, the question of how we knew someone was always confounding; there was rarely a clear and easy answer. I often knew of people before I met them; I often met people in person only to later realize I knew them in another context.

His friend's eyes lit up. Oh, he said, with recognition. It's a pleasure to meet you. He was polite but made me uneasy and I recognized him as the man I'd seen on my morning walk. He'd since shaved and his skin was smooth and clear.

The event was something organized by the municipality, in conjunction with the arts festival. I recognized writers I knew, or knew of, as well as the cool, youngish Bosnian filmmaker who'd been winning all the awards. They were standing in a corner in loose trousers and a white shirt and heavy bangs and eyebrows, fawned over by people twice their age. They looked both uncomfortable with all the attention and as though their life depended on it.

Luka went to get me a drink and I watched him moving away from me. I felt strange, seeing him in his summery, light blue blazer stretched across his shoulders, the particular way he sauntered to the bar, as if I'd experienced that moment before. Ivan remained, his green eyes—so distinct, as though he were wearing eyeliner but I was sure he was not the type of guy to wear eyeliner, there was nothing gender-bending about him—darting across the terrace, fixating on a woman standing near the bar, with her back to us. She wore a gray dress and her hair was long and shiny and I realized it was Marta, the young translator whose debut novel I'd seen at the shop. I hadn't officially met her and at first had not recognized her; usually around the center she wore her hair messily piled atop her head and dressed in pajama pants and large T-shirts, and we kept different hours.

Ivan was watching me now, even though it was his gaze that had led me to Marta. You've known Luka a long time, he said. His accent was difficult to pinpoint, a British-inflected-but-not-quite accent that could make him from anywhere. I heard the Slavic buried below it. He seemed to enjoy being unplaceable.

For a while, I said.

You're one of the translators, he said. He seemed at turns both engaged and preoccupied as we chatted, the kind of person who tries to assess your importance at an event before deciding whether to commit his attention. What had that cold stare been, earlier? I knew he was angry about something that had nothing to do with me. But what. Was someone supposed to meet him? A secret tryst? A morning run, a case of a missed alarm clock as opposed to any sort of broken promise?

Ivan was telling me about a party that he and Luka were attending later that evening. You needed a boat to get there, and though I did not understand if this meant a ten-minute ride or a two-hour tour, I did understand then that Ivan was the type of person who wanted to make sure everyone knew he owned a boat.

Luka then returned with some sort of amaro drink for me, and I thanked him and took a sip. We moved away from the crowd a bit, back toward the terrace's edge.

Still your drink? he asked. It was a good drink but had never been my drink, had it? Again I could have corrected him, out of Ivan's earshot, just the two of us. But I didn't.

Those hot afternoons we used to meet in Athens I generally drank iced espresso, or round after round of tall glasses of beer that never stayed cold enough. We talked mostly of novels. He did not want to write fiction in English, he had then told me. He admired those writers who wrote in a second or third language and recognized the power and liberation of doing so, but he needed his first language for imagination and obligation and a nostalgia to write against.

His journalism was always in English, he had said, and I'd asked if it was because it had more reach, and he'd said, partially. English was the language of power and he wanted to choose his words in ways that had meaning, to resist the passive voice and refuse to make things safe and palatable. English was too ready to cover the horror of its own empire. He wrote in English to fight English's manner of revising, of holding power, of not seeing things as they were. English, he added, gave us the term "balkanization," didn't it?

Every so often I'd be surprised to see him on the news; in a BBC clip from a protest in Sarajevo, or reporting on North Macedonia and the significance of names.

This party, I began to glean, had to do with the play that was premiering that night, which I had planned to attend with the other translators. We would go that night, to the amphitheater nearby.

A new translation of Beckett's *Happy Days* into Croatian, by a translator at the center who stood across the terrace with another translator in residence, Alexandra, who was dating the actor who played Winnie. I had seen the three of them that morning when I returned from my walk, sitting on our large shared terrace, drinking coffee in the early sun.

Now, at the party, on the terrace, Alexandra's girlfriend—she had introduced her simply as K.—was standing with a man I would later recognize as the actor playing Willie, appropriately enough. Here above the buried earth they seemed nearly ethereal. His eyes were round and brown and his brow heavy, like Winnie's. They could have been siblings. You could tell they were only making a quick appearance before they'd disappear, to prepare for the evening, in whatever way actors prepared.

Everyone seemed transfixed by them, and they moved through the party as though they were both the stars and passersby. Alexandra, who translated from English to Greek, recognized me from across the terrace and waved. Had we all planned to meet here and I had forgotten?

Ivan touched my forearm. Have we met before?

Could be, I said.

Pretty necklace, he said, gesturing to my throat.

Thanks, I said. A gift. I drew my hand to it, a small evil-eye pendant, having forgotten I was wearing it.

From someone special, he said, as if he'd known me for years. I did not like this type of fishing so I raised my eyebrows and said nothing.

You missed the presentations, he added, meaning, as I understood it, that this party had begun with a literary event. He gestured to a small area in the corner of the terrace, set up with lines of white chairs, a podium. This contributed to the wedding effect. I saw the poster, now, adorned with Luka's face and several others.

Natalia, Ivan said. Natalia in the navy-blue dress.

But I was not wearing a navy-blue dress.

WAS I NATALIA IN THE NAVY DRESS? I DID NOT DENY IT, I did not correct him; I had allowed for the merging of character and self and maybe I'd even craved it. Luka had translated how he saw me, a version of me that belonged to me but also did not. A version that belonged to him. I sat with this a moment. A version that belonged to him. No. That wasn't quite right.

From what I understood, Ivan had connected me to a character in Luka's book, a book that had not yet been published but that I surmised he had read from, there at the festival, and then I had walked right in, as if the scene he'd read were continuing on.

Most translators will agree that translation is not transfer but interpretation; some translators go so far as to say that translators are editors too. I agree. I wondered if I wanted not to disappear but to be recast. Neither active nor passive but something in between. I was going to disappear into the action as it acted upon me.

Natalia in the navy dress. I glanced down, for a moment actually having forgotten what I was wearing. The lilac-and-red-patterned sundress I'd bought in the dead of winter, when buying such a ridiculously joyful thing felt like a promise of summer. Large, poppy-like flowers. Anyway, I loved the dress. I was relieved to be wearing it, even though something had come unhinged: another self in another reality, cast out to tell another story.

Marta joined our conversation and asked if I'd been to the olive groves and vineyards on the other side of the island, or the nearby old city, once an ancient Greek settlement. Because I was still mulling something over I must have seemed to be looking elsewhere, staring blankly, then slowly adjusting my eyes to her face.

You okay? she asked.

I told her I had not, but I was planning on it. She had not been either, but within the city itself was a church of the patron saint of dogs and below it the ancient Roman baths. A baroque palace, and a fortified villa of a poet, with twenty sayings carved into the walls. A town of inscriptions.

I mentioned I was thinking of renting a bicycle to visit. I don't know why I said this; I didn't really enjoy biking and knew it had to be a very long and hilly ride. Luka looked at me oddly when I said this, and said, We can go if you like. Sunday.

I liked ruins as much as the next person, I supposed, and there'd always been a comfortable familiarity between Luka and me, one that seemed to survive distance and time.

We had more drinks. Soon, it was time to go to the play.

OUTSIDE THE AMPHITHEATER, THE MOOD WAS BRIGHT, the setting sun still kissing noses, faces, washing everyone in an elegant softness. Beautifully dressed people were being photographed as though it were the Oscars. I found my translators and they joined my ragtag bunch from the rooftop. Luka sat to one side, Alexandra to the other, and Marta and Ivan down the row.

I watched the actors on the stage and projected on the screen above it, with English subtitles. Had the play been translated back into English or was the original English version used? Had the translator worked from English or French? I had a program and fumbled in my bag for my glasses, which I'd left in my room.

There were gorgeous hills around the amphitheater, and I'd heard there were strategic places you could gather to watch if you didn't have a ticket.

I was enjoying the play, which I had last seen years ago in Athens during its summer festival, but the setting here somehow seemed perfect for it, the way we sat on the stone steps of the amphitheater, as if in the dirt near the two actors, as if at any moment we could all be buried in piles of dirt too. The production used its setting, the ruins of the old amphitheater, as part of the set, so there was a sense of the audience being part of the show.

Winnie's chatter, her need for ritual, the despondency, something about it made my heart race. During a moment in the second act, I looked at Luka's profile, his large, straight, handsome nose, and imagined him buried in that hole next to me.

And the mound of the sand, it felt like too much, like I could feel it on my skin. The claustrophobia, unbearable. I had to get out of my chair. I whispered to Alexandra—beaming at her Winnie, who was mesmerizing—and then to Luka that I would be back and I didn't answer either when they asked me what was wrong. Marta glanced up as I left. Luka looked as though he was going to follow me but I waved my hand for him to stay seated.

In the concessions area, beneath a trellis, I gulped down a glass of sparkling water the bartender poured for me, let him pour me another, and walked over to a high cocktail table, where I leaned with my head in my hands, feeling wobbly. Too much to drink, not enough to eat. The man brought me a small bowl of tiny crackers. I ate them and downed the water and walked out to the front entry gates, now less agitated.

The area was empty, except for an usher or two, and one teenage boy talking on his phone. His date had stood him up, it seemed, and he was angrily telling a friend about it.

As I approached the door, I met the eyes of a woman in a navy-blue dress, the only other person in the lobby aside from the staff. She was also moving quickly to the outside, as if about to take a phone call. She smiled at me, distantly.

I did the same. She smoked near the other entrance, her back to me, kicking at the ground absent-mindedly. I used the restroom. As I was walking back into the theater, I saw the woman reentering, as if we were mirroring the other. Her long hair was tied back in a ponytail that swished back and forth, back and forth.

I approached an usher and told him I was not feeling well, could I stand there, in the aisle, and he didn't seem to care. I was relieved when the play was over, when the audience emptied back out. I looked for the woman in the navy dress but didn't see her. I pulled my hair back off my face, into a ponytail, and I found my group. The moon was big and bright, and I felt at ease again, for a while.

TOGETHER WE WALKED THOSE DARK, COZY STREETS, HEADing to dinner. Luka had been particularly struck by the play; he'd never seen or read it before—he said this with a bit of shame and also I was sure that he had, I remembered he'd been in Athens when it was performed—and he was going on about sorrow and middle age. He kept repeating that line of the play, then translating it to English: *Sorrow keeps breaking in.* I knew he had experienced his share of it—beyond sorrow, profound losses, the terror of war and genocide in a country that was still healing and a world that still used its geographical locale to speak of barbarous fracture. I also knew he did not like to talk of it.

Sorrow keeps breaking in. That's middle age, Luka was saying to Marta, as if middle age were a little-known concept that needed explanation, but she laughed, saying, I know something about middle age.

Thirties are not middle age, he said, and I laughed out loud.

I should have chimed in but I didn't; it's only men and young people who are allowed to talk about aging without being considered pathetic. I mean, I disagree, but I was so used to younger people so quickly unsexing older ones that I didn't want to bother. If you abstained from all the things that made women look like all the other women their age, and therefore appropriate, you were somehow inappropriate. I was aging and therefore inappropriate. And wasn't this dismissal of women of a certain age a kind of misogyny, a projection to a self at a later date, a self from whom we all hid? As I moved through life, I became aware of a reaction to my own living, a shame I'd register from the quick glance of a male acquaintance I hadn't seen in years, surprised to find that I, too, had aged along with him, and that this was a moral failing, this loss, first of youth, then of youthfulness.

I myself had thought that word, "youthful," when I saw Alexandra's girlfriend that morning on the terrace, a word of course we never use for the young.

Middle age, Luka was saying. The right road lost.

The right road lost in a dark wood seemed a narrow way to think about it: What, after all, was the right road? No, I said. More like a road we veered off from violently, a road we tore up with a jackhammer.

It's not that I no longer felt sadness: for the world and for losses and for bad choices and for those who had hurt me and whom I had hurt. Of course I did. But it no longer felt like a cage that would never, ever lift, never let me out. I had been conditioned to think that menopause would be an end, but it was a reset. A beginning of a story that starts in the middle. The word "pause" implies "to be continued." I had entered a story in its middle. I did not feel like a dried-out husk of myself or that I was slowly disappearing but instead like I'd become part of a larger space, a larger feeling, as if the boundaries of my self had opened up. I no longer needed to assert a self, or forgo one. Something else.

A beginning atop a beginning atop a mound of earth, and everything buried there. Sure, there were the challenges of a changing body. Yet I felt like I'd done an open-water swim, from one island to the next, and now stood looking out across the sea. Singing and triumphant.

I watched Luka, his gentle, playful manner, telling a story to the group. Everyone was laughing at something, and I joined them.

That night went on and on, beginnings accumulating atop beginnings, like a terraced hill, like a vertical history built into the landscape, complete with dreams.

Something of me had come productively unhinged.

ONE OF THE ACTORS WAS TALKING WITH LUKA AND IVAN now, with the sort of playful flirtation of having known one another a while. Marta, I could tell, was aware of Ivan. She watched them both and then turned to me. Are you in love with Luka?

I'm sorry? But then I laughed. She was so frank! Are you?

No, she said. His reading was so sad. *Natalia*, she said, and at first I thought she was addressing me, but I understood it to be the title of his book. She reached into her tote bag, retrieved another pair of shoes, and removed one heel at a time, slipping her feet into sneakers. Much better, she said. You've known him awhile? she asked.

Yeah, I said. I was distracted, though, by her comment about his sad reading. Are you in love with Ivan? I asked instead.

Not anymore, she said. She asked what I was working on, and I told her as much as I knew thus far: A woman whose good friend becomes obsessed with a biologist many years younger than he is. The woman listens to him, mostly over coffees in a small bar in Athens, and then when he leaves, she retells the story to us, her own interpretation.

It sounds good, she said. What's the title?

Occupation, I told her, deciding how to translate it on the spot. Though *Occupation* was more accurate, I had thought of it as *Possession*. This was less accurate to me but somehow more precise; but there was the very famous novel in English of that title already. "Occupation" had with it in English its own conceptual and historical baggage, and when I had to voice it to a listener, *Occupation* was the obvious choice, and I think the right one.

As we neared the restaurant I stopped at a pharmacy, told the others I'd find them. My mouth tasted like cigarettes. Had I smoked at lunch? I could see myself, now, seated at the end of the table, laughing, with a cigarette. I remembered why I'd quit, two decades before, and why I'd kept quitting for a decade after that.

I bought a toothbrush and a small tube of toothpaste, and when I arrived at the restaurant, I brushed my teeth in the bathroom. A young couple all over each other, in heels and shiny dresses, came in laughing, pretending not to notice me grooming myself in public, but I felt better. Then one started to apply mascara to the other's eyes. In the mirror I looked the same. There was a red mark on my forehead, from I don't know what, like I'd walked into a door (had I?). My eyes, though, were clear and bright. In that light they almost looked golden, like a cat's.

These are not gaps in my memory as I recollect that night because one of the things I remember so clearly is that eerie gap, that sense of having lost time, the sense of unreality.

I hovered awkwardly over the toilet, buzzed enough to feel unsteady. Narration is a translation too. I translate you to create you, I said out loud to no one. The music from the previous day's concert played through my mind, and I was reminded both of a café that was close to my former campus in the States and of the time I'd spent here in this country years ago. The music also reminded me of both the Ukrainian songs my grandmother used to sing to me and the Greek folk songs I learned as a child.

Now these soundtracks had cleaved, becoming a strange sound of safety and relief and a third thing I could not name.

THE RESTAURANT WAS OUTDOORS, GARDEN STYLE, WITH little white lights strewn about. When I walked to the table, I heard Luka call to me. Natalia, he said, waving. Over here, he said, and I marveled at how natural it felt to be this woman, to answer to this name. Sit by me, Marta said, and pulled up a chair between herself and Ivan. At first I'd thought Marta was eyeing Ivan with jealousy, but it was now clear she felt relieved to be out of his line of sight. At the other end of the table was a Scandinavian writer named Lena. Most of the other writers and translators were either from southeast Europe or translating into or from these languages. Lena's work must have been translated into a Balkan language, or maybe her success in Europe was so great that she'd been invited simply for her status.

She was not a translator, at least not one staying at the center, there were only fifteen of us, but she seemed to know a lot of the writers—seemed very aware of Ivan's gaze, seemed to be performing for it, taking out a cigarette and staring out across the garden, quite sure she was being watched. She and Marta seemed aware of each other too.

Over the chatter of how much to order, were we drinking wine or rakija, others said it was hot and they wanted beer. Beer's good, I agreed. I asked Marta about what she was working on at the center but she said she was too superstitious to talk about her work, which I understood. Though I think she didn't want Ivan to hear. She seemed preoccupied, though not as drunk as the others—everyone seemed to have been drinking through the play. I had already moved through drunkenness once and it seemed like it was about to begin again, sudsing up like shampoo.

Marta reached into her giant bag and plopped her own novel onto the table. I'd like to give this to you, she said to me. I told her that was so kind, that I had meant to buy it earlier. I'd like you to have this one, she said. I asked her to sign it for me.

Where's my signed copy? Ivan asked. He was smiling, had his arm stretched behind my chair. He leaned over to touch Marta's shoulder. Normally I would have leaned forward but I stayed there, an obstruction. He irritated me.

You don't have a copy? Marta asked. At first, her voice was playful. To the untrained ear.

Ivan shrugged. I was waiting for you to give me one.

It's been out for three months, Marta said. Go into any bookshop, here, London, Paris. Luka has read it, she continued, gesturing at him.

Luka caught my eye and held it a moment.

Why haven't you? I asked Ivan, trying to sound playful.

Yeah, Ivan, Luka said, gently, trying to assuage some hurt feelings, to de-escalate. Whatever had happened between them, there had been a lot of hurt.

Marta flagged the server down and asked for a beer, and then looked around the table and asked for several. Ivan was stunned, so used to being the object of her attention, not her rage. She, I gleaned, had often been the object of his rage. When she voiced her feelings, either they were ignored or, more likely, she was chastised for them. In turn, she'd spend the next few hours or days consoling him and apologizing some more because her feelings had hurt his. I imagined she apologized frequently and he, never.

How did I know this? Well, I didn't. But I had a hunch.

Marta lurched forward, close to the table, to move her body from Ivan's, as if he repulsed her. Then she began taking items from her large handbag, looking for a pen. A phone, a wallet, a packet of tissues, various lip balms and makeup and a bottle of water and a copy of Luka's first book in its first original and also the book of the British writer, who had not shown. Post-it notes sticking out from the pages. A pack of cigarettes. I mean, she must have been aware of what she was doing, it was all very slow and dramatic. She seemed very drunk, but suddenly, as though everything from that long day had decided to process through her body, as if it had been waiting in some holding tank. Because I'm American, and because of the play of course, there I was waiting for a gun, for it to come out of the bag after the small eyeshadow palette.

Marta? I asked, and I felt strange, as though I were hearing myself speak, felt my face go a little numb. My voice both sound and echo, both call and response. I could hear myself talking but slowed down. I don't know what happened after that, but later Luka told me I'd passed out right there, my head lolling onto the table.

Natalia, Luka said.

I WAS WALKING ALONG A RIVER. THIS WAS THE IMAGE THAT played through my mind, these were the words I heard in a symphony of languages. No. Language, then something, then language.

To agree, in Greek, is to be aligned in voice.

Natalia, Natalia. I could hear his voice, but I walked steadily along the river's bank. Purple flowers, the sour figs that grew over rock.

If memory lives in the body, what happens when the body slips into something new, when its borders open up to the land and sea that surround it? Not buried in the earth but very much alive? What vessel houses our memories, our thoughts, or do they drift and stream out after us, disembodied now, part of the space around us, both visible and invisible? Or is memory simply intuition? Isn't this how works of art are made? We create things to imagine a future and a time before we existed. The present leaves a mark on the past, and memory sometimes works in more than one direction.

The new original changes the old.

When I finally opened my eyes, I was surrounded by concerned faces. I brought my hand to my head, which was pounding.

Do we need a doctor? Luka asked.

No, I said. I'm okay.

Marta said, Let's go to the bathroom. We stood up at the same time and she took me by the elbow. At the sink, I splashed water on my face and insisted I was fine. Then, we sat outside at a small grouping of chairs, probably set up for the staff to take cigarette breaks. Marta said she and Luka and Ivan had been on a panel together earlier that day, before the party, and

Lena, the woman who was seated at our table, had asked her a question that had made her livid, though I couldn't follow what had happened.

A man walked out of the restroom and she asked him politely for a cigarette. He smiled and lit it for her, ate her with his eyes, as they say in Greek. I declined.

I don't usually smoke, she said.

Of course, I said. I don't mind. Women in American novels always begin to smoke as a sign of rebellion, I added.

She laughed. That's the best we can come up with? She waved her cigarette in the air and continued, telling me that Ivan wasn't really invited, not by the festival, but since he has a home nearby he acts entitled to all of it. He ran a small, respected press in France. They'd published her French translation, but she didn't say if she'd met him that way and I didn't ask.

I didn't realize you lived in France, I said.

Yeah, she said. For years, in Paris. I live in Zagreb now. I prefer it. I can live off my writing, mostly. You live in the States?

I paused, thinking about how to answer this. Not anymore, I said. I haven't lived in the States for a few years now.

She told me about the English-language travel magazine she wrote for, the various editorial jobs she picked up. I don't know where he gets his money, she added, and I could tell that "he" referred to Ivan.

I nodded but didn't say anything. That explained his accent, sort of European but not particularly rooted to any one language or place.

Marta took a mirror from her bag and held it up to reapply her lipstick.

When I met him years ago, she said, through mutual friends, he wanted to be a writer. I was young and smitten. I read every single thing he wrote, sometimes several times. He showered me with attention. Except when I sent him something of mine. He'd rarely even mention it.

That's shitty, I said.

Like maybe this is my sort of resistance, she said.

I was not following—what was "this"? What was her resistance? But I let her go on.

Someone in the audience said my work was too concerned with men. "Male-identified." She rolled her eyes. I mean, look at the culture I grew up in. She waved her cigarette in front of her again. Even if I write the men completely out of my stories, what's the difference, they do all the harm anyway.

Marta continued, pulling her hair into a bun and then pulling it back out. And if I write a novel about a woman talking to another woman about art or politics or another woman or ice cream and not about a man? Will that change anything?

Maybe, I said. No?

Marta took a brush out of her bag and ran it through her hair violently. Then she reapplied lipstick.

You should write what you like to write, I said.

Because what they are saying, Marta continued, is that I am too concerned with men. With being desired. But that's not true. It isn't. Sure, we talk about men, we talk about love. So? She stood up to head back to the table and then turned back to me. Ivan, she said, is the kind of guy who would divert a river for his own needs.

I picked up the small mirror and looked at my face. Was I as drunk as she was?

Oh, Jesus, I'm sorry, she said. How are you feeling?

Tell me about a complicated woman, I said.

What? But she eased up and laughed. My god, I'm drunk, she said. Maybe you want to rejoin the group?

Sure, I said. Let's.

Has this happened before? she asked.

I wondered about the "this." Unclear antecedent.

Now and again, yeah, I said.

BACK AT THE TABLE, LUKA HANDED ME A TANGERINE-Y soda, which I drank quickly, its taste reminiscent of something from long ago. I felt a burst of affection for him and I dabbed my eyes with a napkin. Though I'd just washed my hands, I applied and reapplied hand sanitizer, a habit that will surely stay with me forever.

The others were laughing and singing. Ivan was smoking and leaning across the table, talking with a writer with long red hair. He glanced up at us. At another table, a group of locals broke into a traditional song, one that many around us seemed to know. I asked Luka about the music from the day before, trying to reproduce the song's melody. I was surprised by how easily it rose from my throat into the air. Language lives in layers inside us, stratified and petrified, bubbling up here and there, like those ancient buried rivers poised to flood.

How do you know those lyrics? he asked.

I didn't know the lyrics, just a few of the lines. They'd been printed on the program in several languages, and I had read what I could of all of them.

Luka told me that the name for this genre of music came from the word for melancholy, that it was about leaving one's home, and exile, and a longing for a place that no longer existed. I told him Greece had such songs too, how deeply I felt the music in my body. It was melancholy yet it made me want to belt it out, get up and dance. How familiar the music was. Good music moved through the body, and my body marked the boundary between places.

Remember, I said. I've lived here before.

Have you, he said, and smiled. It's usually tourists who love this music.

That was when Winnie and Willie arrived at the taverna. Everyone stood up and clapped.

Marta now sat at the end of our table, where a crowd of younger people had packed in closely, layers of them. I recognized a few other translators.

Luka asked if I was okay.

I think I should turn in, I said.

I'll walk you there.

BACK AT THE TRANSLATORS' CENTER, I COULD HEAR VOICES toward the back of the terrace, talking and laughing. Two older translators, a Bosnian and a Bulgarian, were in the small library with the windows closed, smoking, which was a peculiar choice, considering the ratio of outdoor space to indoor space. They were watching something on television and laughing.

Luka never seemed in a hurry, never seemed to want to be anywhere except where he was. I always liked this about him. He did not seem to want to go back to the group, or to go home—he said he had a small place outside of town. During all these years of our friendship he had walked me home many times, and it did not feel odd or suggestive. What did he see when he looked at me? A character in his imagination or me, the woman walking beside him? Natalia or me or someone else entirely?

Luka followed me into the large shared kitchen and we both peered inside the fridge.

I took a soda water and told Luka I had some warm ones in my room, because I suddenly remembered that's how he drank it.

Perfect, he said.

I'll be right back, I said, but he was following me up the stairs.

I asked Luka if he had a translator yet, into English, and he said he didn't; the book would not be out until late that summer. Interested? he asked, and there was something impish in his eyes.

What would it be like to translate *Natalia*? Would I be flat or full, in my own control? How would my own hand change the story, ineffably, imperceptibly, violently? Would I recognize myself, could I recast a story that was made of my story and words and did not belong to me? Was Natalia a better translation of who I was? Could Luka's rendering contain another equally valid manifestation of me?

Luka always said that writing was a translation of human behavior, and his novel, the way I understood it, seemed to narrate a translated version of me, where some version of myself, a different life, wound tightly with my own. Or maybe a novel that recognized something already inside me. I was living in this middle voice, both the actor and acted upon. I was both the smuggler and the smuggled. How had this changed me, the woman Luka was following up the stairs, and the woman who now tells this story? That was the question.

Another time Luka and I had crossed paths had been at a literary festival in Thessaloniki, where I was on a panel for my first novel, which had just been published in Greek, but not yet in English. The novel was set in Athens, during the military dictatorship there in the late 1960s and early 1970s. I noticed Luka in the audience and he gave me a warm smile.

But in the Q&A portion, Luka's hand went up. He said: You are exploring a very painful history that you did not live. What makes you think you have this right?

It felt like a power move, a challenge. I knew Luka understood what fiction was. He was not saying one should only write autobiographically, which I never did. Not what was my right, but what did it mean. I had done my research, I had been studious, but maybe had not considered enough of what it meant to write into another painful collective history, or to be somehow drawn to the narratives of catastrophe, even though I would not have admitted it then. I used to think of narrative as something to shore things up, but now I understand all the things it can obscure. Narratives of self, narratives of nation.

There had been an interpreter translating into Greek, but I answered in Greek, which threw the interpreter off. It's a good question, I said, and I'm not sure it's a question of rights.

Luka did not let me continue, or give my answer in English. But where are you in this story? Where is your Americanness?

I don't remember what I answered, but since then I have been answering him in my mind. I had always found politics and literature to be inextricable, yet I had failed to consider the politics of my own subjectivity. I can imagine the irony he saw that I did not.

Though these questions were already swirling through the discourse, they had not yet become prevalent. Luka was really not the type to ask such an aggressive question; he was the type to assert that art was art and it was always morally complicated, so I know something in my presentation had really touched a nerve. But shouldn't a writer be able to answer that question? If I could go back to anything I've ever written, I'd change everything. I am always returning to the same unsteady terrain. Then again, do we have to be transparent about where we are in a story? On that I am not so sure.

Later, though, he apologized. In my mind, it was after that that we became closer friends. An acknowledgment of something. Of difference? But I may be remembering incorrectly: It's possible we had already been friends but that he could never have asked me something so painful in private. That is, it's possible it was because of our friendship that he needed the public buffer. Did he remember this moment at all?

Because after that, my voice felt blocked, buried deep inside me. Other books were written but unpublished, books without bindings. Mounds of dirt without an oar. The process of writing for me was kaleidoscopic, stories that shifted and changed and became brighter and more muted, every story merging into the next. Write and erase, write and erase. I sometimes think everything I write is a revision of the last thing, my words on a continuum bound only by the boundaries of the object, the physical book.

Translation allowed me the pleasure to step out of that, to construct a narrative outside this continuum. To step, with permission, into another person's words. Not to create a narrative but to coax it out.

BACK IN MY ROOM, THE SWEATER I'D MEANT TO BRING along with me was on the bed, as were my reading glasses and lipstick and a balled-up wad of cash I'd meant to transfer to my handbag. I opened the lipstick; it had melted and mashed. I threw it out. My laptop was open, and my notebook beside it, and I'd left the shutters to the balcony undrawn. It looked like I'd just left the room to go downstairs for a coffee; it had the feeling of being recently abandoned. How much time had passed, really?

I sat on the bed. Luka sat next to me, put his hand to my forehead.

I'm fine, I said.

Luka's phone rang, and I walked out to the balcony.

A few minutes later, I heard him call to me, Natalia, asking if I was okay. I recalled a bedroom, rising from the bed to open the shutters, Luka handing me a glass of water, a hairbrush, telling me about the jugo wind that turns the sea hazy and green and the north wind, with its waters blue and clear. *The North Wind's breath will blow the ship.*

In the hallway, others were going to their rooms, drunk and talking loudly. Do you want to take that bike ride on Sunday? he asked, and I told him, No, I don't know why I said I'd bike.

Let's take a water taxi instead, he said.

Not too early, I added, and he laughed. I know, Natalia, he said. Remember?

Of course I had no idea what he was talking about. From my balcony I watched him leaving down the narrow street, probably heading to join Ivan at that party. When he got to the corner, he turned back to face me, just before he disappeared from view. I'm not sure he saw me there but he waved, held his hand up, just in case.

I was looking forward to Sunday.

If you looked to the left, you could see a sliver of the water, so close. Though I could not see the terrace, I could hear laughter still coming from it, some music. The flower moon shone over the flat mirror of the sea. Diving in would shatter the glass.

II

Anne Carson writes: "Decreation is an undoing of the creature in us—that creature enclosed in self and defined by self. But to undo self one must move through self, to the very inside of its definition."

Since I was a child, I've had nightmares of annihilation. Though they disappeared in my twenties, they resurfaced in my thirties, and in my forties they became frequent. Sometimes they were tied to world events; other times to stresses at work, in life. For a long time they involved being trapped inside a space invaded by groups of men; others involved fires, or air raids.

I've read that inherited trauma can skip a generation, and I surmised that the dreams belonged to my maternal grandmother, a woman who could only drink to obliterate the pain, obliterate herself. Though I was neither in the country of my birth nor in the one I called home, I could feel some wounded history running below the clean, holiday-town cheerfulness. Something buried in the language, buried in me.

The man on the ferry had been unsettling because his anger had seemed so directed at me, and also mistaken. His lurching at me with his car. Yet now I thought I'd been uneasy the entire time I had talked with my friend, or even boarding the ferry on that hazy morning.

I've had this feeling from time to time, right before something bad, or unsettling, happened. A few years before, I'd left my night class and walked to the parking lot with that feeling of unease. Something menacing. My class had gone well, and besides the fact that I was walking alone in the dark, nothing in particular had happened to make me feel unsafe. Five minutes later, on a stretch of dark road between campus and the expressway, I was carjacked.

They, two young men, pulled me out of the car, but other than that, they did not hurt me, and one—I remember his bright green eyes—actually helped me steady myself after he pulled too hard, surprised and frightened by himself, like a fawn at the side of the road. It felt like they realized that what they were going through all that trouble for was silly, but they couldn't stop.

I was telling this all to Luka over beers, a few nights after the Beckett play, recalling details I had until then forgotten. Like: They wore surgical masks and scrubs, like med students, though they must have had jackets; it was a spring cold snap, barely thirty degrees. I recognized their accents as from the east-side suburbs, not the ones along the lake but the ones northeast of the city, strip malls and car dealerships and old diners that had been there since the 1920s. My car was a twelve-year-old Toyota and not exactly on the prized possession list.

Rookies, I said, and Luka laughed, uncomfortably. You don't have to make light of it, he said. It's okay.

I raised my glass, and he raised his, and we toasted. To what I don't know.

Honestly, I said, I was so startled, I thought it was a prank. Some kind of dare.

I continued: I never drive wearing a coat and my car sped away with my coat in the back (and maybe this is why in my mind they are also not wearing jackets). I walked past a stretch of field. A row of houses but no lights, and a coffee shop that closed at five. The athletic field and a parking lot. There was a light dusting of snow, which would normally not drive everyone inside, but it was April.

Snow in April! said Luka. He reached across the table and touched my hand.

I walked half a mile and called the police from inside an old, big house turned café called Zora Rose. A review might call it eclectic. Good Balkan and Eastern Mediterranean food, live music some nights; Greek and Armenian, Arabic and Bosnian and Turkish music. Multiracial, multiethnic, multigenerational. Very young people, student types, and older jazz musicians and locals who'd probably lived in the neighborhood for years.

Sounds nice, Luka says.

I must have looked wretched when I walked in because the bartender was looking at me with concern, and another young woman approached me quickly. I explained what had happened, and she took my arm and led me to the bar. The bartender gave me his hoodie and brought me tea, and the young woman returned with a bowl of beef and bean soup. The bartender asked: Who would do this to you? And I admitted I did not know.

That night, it was pretty quiet, but the musicians were playing, two young men and a woman with a clear, lilting voice. I hadn't thought of it this way then, but that experience marked a distinct turn, a pivot, a beginning of a story after which so much else followed.

Despite the distress of what had happened, I felt such relief and safety in that music café, and I felt myself relax telling Luka about it. It must have been the music I'd listened to the previous week that caused me to recollect, because what remained clearly in my memory was that hour I'd spent in the café, regaining my bearings, listening to the musicians, recovering, eating soup

And my burned-out taillight disappearing down the road, as if I were watching myself speed away.

AT THE TRANSLATORS' RESIDENCE, WE SETTLED INTO ROUTINE.

Several of us, the translators, those next few nights after the play, had dinner together, and each night when we returned around ten or eleven, the younger translators were gathering in the sitting room, about to go out. It gave the place an interesting feeling of shifts, of rhythms, a constant ebb and flow like the tide, and came with the realization that I was no longer one of the younger ones, staying out all night. I preferred to get up before dawn, not return then. Marta and I were the only two translating into English—she translated both from Croatian and Bosnian, and I from Greek—and it was clear from the beginning that our conversations would only use English when there was no other commonality between us, even if our fluencies were not perfect. So sometimes at a dinner, conversations were happening in various Balkan languages, or French or German or Italian.

Often my afternoon coffee break in the shared kitchen coincided with their breakfast, which was why I was surprised to find Marta there one early morning, hovering like a kestrel, waiting for the kettle. I'd come back from my morning swim, showered, and was about to make myself a coffee.

She looked as though she'd been crying.

Can't sleep, she said.

I understand, I said.

She assembled her tea, and I put some cookies on a plate, along with a few apricots. Drink your tea and eat something, sometimes that helps, I said.

I thought she'd take it all back to her room, but instead she moved from the table to the couch, holding her tea close to her face. Her demeanor had shifted, and gone was that brash outspokenness I'd witnessed on that long night out.

I felt for her; I remembered myself in this state.

She was curious about the novel I was translating, so I told her more: The man is a filmmaker and the young woman a biologist he met while making a film about the Eleonora's falcon, named, according to the novel, after Eleanor of Arborea, a Sardinian judge who, in the late fourteenth century, passed a law that protected birds' nests against illegal hunters.

The novel's narrator has been friends with the man since they were young, but because the biologist's research is on the island the narrator is from, she begins to know her too.

I trailed off because I didn't yet know what else happened; I was so early in the writing that I was relying on what the book jacket said.

Those falcons are here too, Marta said. She placed her mug on the table, reclined on the couch, and closed her eyes. I don't want to go to my room, she said.

I felt uneasy leaving her to nap and cry on the couch in the shared public space, so I retrieved my laptop and notebooks from my room and worked for a while at that large table. I found a blanket in the shared linen closet and covered her. She fell asleep almost immediately.

Others drifted in and out and looked at me quizzically, gesturing to Marta. Another translator, Irini, came in and said they had been out late. She made some tea, ate one of the apricots, then disappeared to her room.

The year I turned forty, an older friend told a mutual friend that she thought I was unhappy. She'd said it with judgment, as if emotions were the same as moral flaws, as if I were somehow an affront to her. I thought of Brookner, that a woman's melancholia was "less picturesque" than a man's, "an affliction too serious to be put into words." But my friend was not wrong: At the time I had felt reckless, nearly out of my mind with fury. I didn't realize I'd begun that transit of perimenopause quite early, as had my grandmother, another way it felt my body was reenacting something in hers, a sort of backward imprinting, generational progression that forgets which way to move, a sense of time moving in two directions. Something in my grandmother imprinted inside my mother, inside her uterus, or maybe something of what would be me imprinted there too.

But then one night, over a late-night dinner at a cozy taverna, my friend who'd mentioned my unhappiness confessed her own struggles; she'd recognized something of her younger self in me. Then we drank a lot of wine and she told me and two other unsuspecting friends, all of us in our early forties then, what would happen to our bodies, our vaginas, how age would devastate them. That was the word she'd used. "Devastate." She was going through a lot. But I don't think we were ever the same.

Around nine Marta woke again and poured herself some sparkling water from the fridge. She made herself an espresso, and made a second for me.

I felt a tenderness toward her, a swift urge to protect her from what was ahead: to prepare her for the future restlessness and recklessness I knew might soon come and invite her to tear up her life. At least, what had come to mine.

Yeah, she said. She gestured to my notebook. Are you writing your translation? she asked. I'd love to hear the opening.

So I read it to her, just the first few pages. And when those words I'd written but also had not written moved through my body, I had to fight the desire to add moments that weren't there, to digress when there were no digressions, to add my own narrative commentary, though of course I did not. Yet— and I'm not sure I can explain why—I felt the writer had placed a chair in the corner of the text for me, the translator, to sit in. My own occupation of the work. That the work itself invited and challenged the question of translation, wondering what I'd do when I wandered around that space.

I was not the narrator yet I was both instrument and score. Voice that emerged, anew, neither mine nor hers but combinatory, the porous border between us that defined the text.

IN THAT ROCKY ADRIATIC COVE, NOT FAR FROM WHERE tourists departed in the high season to visit the caves, I swam each morning, very early, which gave each day a new, refreshed quality. I was hesitant because I did not know these waters as well, if you can ever really know waters at all. I didn't know how far out I could go, when the water became shallow enough to stand, where to avoid the sea urchins, and so on. Still, sometimes, I felt the waters I knew swirling around me.

And: The Adriatic flowed into the Ionian, and only on this side of it, at the top of the sea, did I understand that the Ionian was my emotional home, and though I liked how easily I was connected to it I also imagined being sucked away, a magnet drawing me back, like the sea turtles near my grandparents' home who find the same shore each year to mate, to nest, and those tiny vulnerable hatchlings making their way back to the sea. Like the Eleonora's falcon, flying each year from Madagascar to the Ionian.

Those sunrise swims, another woman always arrived at the same time; we entered the water on opposite sides of the cove almost every morning. Sometimes we waved, other times not. I've been swimming on quiet morning beaches my whole life, and these shared rhythms are nothing unusual. Here, though, because it was still an unfamiliar yet familiar place, I found her presence a comfort.

One morning when she did not come, I felt disoriented. The water was clear and blue, like always. The sun was still gentle and powerful. I swam alone, finally finding my usual rhythm but unusually impatient to finish, imagining my body slicing the border between sea and sky. For a while a school of small barracuda who seemed far too placid for barracuda swam nearby. Three or four white-blue fish seemed to follow me in the water, small fish, curious, as though maybe my body in the water was a sort of shelter. One young octopus, peeking from behind coral, behind rock. A drakaina—I didn't know what its name was in English—half buried on the seafloor. I'd stepped on one years ago, and could still remember that deep, nervy pain that lasted a long time.

As I climbed from the sea, I saw her on the shore, not in her usual spot but as though she were waiting for me to emerge, below an old black pine. It was the first time we had spoken, the first time we'd stood so close.

Did you see the jellyfish? she asked in accented English, smoothing her hair into her bathing cap.

Yesterday she'd seen a jellyfish that was bigger than she was. Not far from your rock, she told me, meaning the rock to which I often swam. She—"she," she said, not "it," which I think was her literal translation but I appreciated this grammar all the same—was orangey pinky brown with tentacles, tentacles a meter long.

I awkwardly removed my swim fins, rinsed them off.

The jellyfish did not sting me, the woman continued. She was looking at me, then I saw two others, in the distance. I wanted to know if you saw her, she continued. If you saw any of them.

I hadn't seen any jellyfish, I told her, and I wondered how she could tell the jellyfish had been looking at her. I told her about the barracuda and the fish and the octopus and the drakaina, which she said here was called a spider-fish. She did not look at me but out into the distance, put her hands on her hips. She seemed to be questioning her own story, her statement almost a challenge, and I wished I could corroborate; but I told her I had not. The water had been very clear. The previous summer in Greece, there had been so many jellyfish that we'd transferred our fears of the virus to fears of these gentle and venomous invertebrates. Large purple ones, the ones that could sting you from ten meters away. I never went to the beach without baking soda, which you were to mix into a paste and place on the sting.

That summer, not far from my father's childhood home, a ship had capsized while being towed west, and the survivors were detained in some warehouse in Kalamata. More than six hundred people died. Many suspected the coast guard had been towing the ship not to safety but to its death. Such cruelty. In my mind I associate that incident with my silly commitment to bringing baking soda to the beach. Our fears are always only relative, I know, but every so often a startling rupture shifts our awareness—this was its own sort of cruelty. Not the rupture but the ways we could move through life, worrying about insignificant things, while the world burned.

I asked if she wanted me to wait on the shore for her, and she said no, it was fine, and I left her the small plastic bag filled with baking soda, and I know what it looked like. She looked at it and laughed.

After all, she said, I wasn't stung yesterday. Have you ever heard of this, to see a jellyfish so close and not be stung?

I shrugged. I had, many times, but I'd also never seen the large, mythic creature she described. The more contact I had with the sea, full of life, the more I saw myself as a guest in their space. I didn't like to think of "nature" as something outside myself, but I didn't like to think of it as something I had full access to either. When I swam, I wanted to merge with the sea, to belong to it. Not representing, but presenting. To return.

I'd read about tiny jellyfish that moved from polyp to adult and sometimes back to polyp again. If stressed by their environment, or hunger, they reverted to a younger state and essentially started again.

How beautiful is this? If only our midlife crises worked like this, keeping us immortal instead of ridiculously and haplessly trying to cheat death. No, not cheat it. Delay it, digress from it. The idea of life as a series of revisions and reconsiderations, regressions and regrowth.

What would become of nostalgia, without regret?

But we cannot be immortal, and death is the only final destination, at least of life in this form. I was not having a midlife crisis, or maybe I had already moved through one. I thought it was a silly term anyway: Life was full of crises. A crisis was a judgment, a turning—etymologically the words were linked. A critical moment in which to pause, to see what might come next. It was not a singular point but a long curving road around a mountain that finally pointed you in an unexpected direction. Not late autumn, the leaves all off the trees, though there was beauty in that image too, but spring, serene and proud and glimmering with new life. I was grateful now, to the friend who'd talked so candidly about the changes to our bodies. I appreciated her candor, but I wish this period of life were not described so violently. Did it have to feel so violent?

How would I have known to expect this, when all that seemed appropriate to talk about were hot flashes, with a dash of dramatic comedy? How could I have known that what would follow would be an opening up to an expanse of very blue sky on a clear, warm day, the melancholia having burned off like a fog?

I changed into dry clothes, zipped up my hoodie, and watched the woman swim until I saw her make her way back to the shore. She waved at me, as if to say, All is good. I waved back.

THOSE DAYS AT THE TRANSLATORS' CENTER FLIPPED BY slowly and steadily like the pages in a book, and despite the strange start of them, they felt calm and restful and luxuriously long. The novel translation accumulated before me, through me, and each day felt like three days crammed into one. I liked all the translators, and we had fun together. Alexandra and I were translation mirrors, she transporting work into Greek and I out of it, and we often consulted one another about connotations and precision, and Ioanna, a vibrant woman who translated from French to Greek and was always up for a party. Despite being the oldest among us, she often stayed out late with the younger ones, and berated us if we retired too early.

I saw Luka often, and no one at the center commented on this new romantic development; I think many of them thought we might have been together all along. I stayed with him some nights. At daybreak I swam in the cove near his place and was back at my desk by eight each morning.

Luka had said of Ivan and Marta: Either you're involved or you're not, that if there will be something between two people, there's the bolt or spark right at the beginning, or else never at all. But I would definitely disagree.

I would say something began two days after the Beckett play, when we visited that ancient Greek settlement, amid the olive trees. A recognition between us, a sense that we'd both entered some sort of transitory space, and that space was something collaborative, recombinant, transformative. Or maybe it had been the uttering of a name, and my acceptance of it.

Our paths had often merged in interesting ways, and we were often, by chance, in the same place. Our history, until now, had mostly been linked through drinks in cities that we were not from, though I was always impressed with the way he could identify a compatriot walking toward him on a crowded Chicago street; he had learned, for better or for worse, to read and identify faces. Luka had a deep sense of intuition, and he paid careful attention. He acted as though we had always been involved, even if not articulated, and I didn't quite understand what he meant but he said things like this, from time to time. That anything that happened was always happening and not happening at once. When a story began depended on the teller of the tale, and nothing more or less.

IN THE LATE AFTERNOONS, MARTA SOMETIMES ASKED TO hear more pages of the novel. I had never written anything before that unfolded and reached someone else's ears so quickly; generally I drafted many versions on my own before showing anyone at all. She hung on to the words as though the characters were her good friends, and though Marta didn't have a childlike demeanor—I learned she was discerning and quiet; people would say she was an old soul—it felt like reading to a child who was grasping my hand and forcibly turning the page, either impatient to get to the end or itching to know what happens next. And it was strange for me, too, to be telling a story whose ending, and significance, I didn't yet know.

One afternoon, Marta asked me what I would do after this, and I told her I had no plans.

You're not going back home?

I said nothing. I shrugged and tried to smile and Marta nodded, recognizing I wasn't ready to talk about it.

What about Luka? she asked.

What about him, I said.

She looked at me as if I might explain, but I couldn't. I didn't know.

Are you heading back to Zagreb? I asked.

She nodded. Yes, she said. It's home now.

I asked her if she still had family there, and she said she didn't anymore. They're all in Chicago, she added.

I suppose I'll go back to Greece, I finally said. I told her about my grandparents' house near the Ionian Sea, and explained I still had trouble calling it my house, had trouble acknowledging that it, in fact, belonged to me. I still felt like a trespasser, like someone only passing through.

Marta said she understood.

For the past five years, I'd rented it out to a French couple who were happy to pay probably more than they should, a couple who'd arrived—coincidentally—just before the lockdowns. They'd meant to stay six weeks. But once they could work from home, they decided to stay. They fell in love with that small town, where they could take walks by the sea, spend time outdoors. I'd hired someone from the town to clean, to tend the garden, but it seemed the couple enjoyed these things too. They took excellent care of the place.

When they arrived, a February nearly five years ago, I'd helped them settle in. The money I made from that helped pay for more repairs, and I also used it to rent smaller spaces when I visited: in Athens, or near my cousin on the island.

Marta nodded. She'd heard that the famous British writer had bought a house in that very town, and I wondered how she knew that. Marta was hoping for some gossip but I didn't have much. I told her something I had until then forgotten. That February, while getting a haircut in a salon on the square—I remember it particularly because it was the last haircut I'd have before the lockdowns began—the stylist informed me the British writer had been in a few days before, getting highlights, chatting in her quite decent Greek, asking about real estate.

She is so fascinating, Marta said. What sort of house did she buy?

I admitted I didn't know.

Would I recognize her in public? Marta asked

I don't know. Probably?

I've heard interviews with her on French radio, she said. Perfect French.

French mother, I said.

She nodded. She gets highlights, Marta said, mostly to herself. Then added: I don't picture her with a body at all.

Sometimes this seemed to me the largest act of liberation for a writer, to be without a body. At least, without a body on display. But what to make of that comment? A sort of unsexing, or maybe an unbranding? The British writer, though, was ten years my senior, so bodylessness at an age women feel invisible felt more complicated.

I thought of the novel where a Brazilian novelist disappears, and her translator drops everything to go to Brazil to find her, searching for clues in her work, which she knows as intimately as a lover might know a body. The last time the novelist was seen, she'd climbed up into a tree, with a cigar, as if a writer's best hope for truly being seen was for her bodied self to disappear, enjoying the pleasures of the body away from the public gaze.

You know why that Lena woman upset me so much?

Why? I asked.

I think there's part of me that would do anything to impress a man. I confused a need for artistic validation, approval, with a need for love.

Don't be so hard on yourself.

She hit a nerve, Marta said. Anyway.

And then Ioanna came down the stairs, in her charming, dramatic way.

Hey, Marta said. You want to go get a beer?

Absolutely, Ioanna said. Let's go!

And so we did.

FOR MANY YEARS, THAT HOUSE IN WHICH MY FATHER WAS born, and which now belonged to me, was falling apart. Property was less an investment in space, as it was in the States, and more an investment in time. The house told a common story of inheritance laws in Greece: If things were not addressed directly, often several cousins owned one house and no one was willing to take full responsibility—or not so much unwilling but also not wanting to step on toes, or not able to agree, or not able to afford to do anything at all. For years after my grandparents died, when I was in college, the house had belonged to many, and no one. These houses cover the countryside, in various stages of decline. Because the house had been such a part of my youth, and because it was a physical touchstone for me, I checked on it for years, keeping it up. I don't think anyone in my family noticed.

I told my cousins, who cared about the place but were overwhelmed with their own homes and families and lives, that I would take care of it, checking on it each time I visited. Different groups of people moved in and out. We called them the renters, but they paid no rent. One family had worked on one of the nearby farms—but they'd moved on. Then a young couple and their infant passed through for three weeks, and before that, two young men. It seemed the house was on a sort of empty-house circuit, passed along by word of mouth. In this way the house always felt open and fluid, its histories mixed and compatible, always a work in progress. And in this way, it both belonged to my family and also did not. Anyway, those who'd passed through had all taken decent care of the place, and I'd often wondered what happened to them all, how and if word got out that the house was no longer on a circuit. Equally intriguing was the way these free renters didn't seem to bother my family too much.

The rules of property and possession intrigued me, the way we made rules to allow us to have the things we shouldn't, or should, depending on whom you ask. And here was an intriguing legal thing: You had to declare the clock.

You had to say, to your family, from this point I am intending to take possession of this house. A sort of oikocolonialism. I see something, I want something, I take it, it's mine. The house was not an ancient artifact, proudly displayed in the British Museum. It was only on loan to me; until then I had only been its caretaker, and maybe because of it I felt less like its owner and more like a timid guest.

From this point I am intending to take possession of the house, I said.

The way the house came to belong to me is a complicated story. But the short version is this: Ten years after I uttered those words, the house, undisputedly, belonged to me. I know it seems odd, but what I felt from my cousins was relief. I overheard an old aunt say, It's a shame, now, that the house belongs to her, and another quip back, At least it looks nice now. And who came after me? The house would simply revert to my cousins when I was gone. In Greece, property was less about profit and more about stewardship. On one level, anyway. But it was not my care of the house or even my childlessness but my Americanness that I think they objected to, the complications that arise between siblings and family when some of us stay and some of us leave. I had not left, but my father had, and for this reason I would always feel those inherited tensions. Once he emigrated for graduate school, he did not often return to Greece; many of those summers during which I stayed with my grandparents, he brought me there reluctantly, then left. He moved further from the country while I became enamored of it.

Then, the summer before I turned forty, I found it empty again. I asked around. The neighbors had said they'd seen no one around for months. I knew it made them anxious, both the itinerant tenants and the houses's shabby state, an eyesore at the edge of the town. I hired someone to refinish the floors, to restore the exterior, and an engineer to assess the structural damage, which was not as bad as it looked. New modern doors and new locks. My then partner and I painted and installed new kitchen cabinets, built shelving and closets from the floor to the ceiling. We rented it out, short term, once in a while, and we stayed there when we could. I think we both imagined retiring there. I think this is what Marta wanted to hear. More backstory.

THINGS WERE EASY BETWEEN US, ME AND LUKA.

He was a warmhearted man and we had things in common and didn't ask each other too many questions. There was no period of awkward or embarrassing or rote seduction, but if there were, it would be like every other tale and not worth repeating. But because of this new status between us, it was difficult for me to remember what things had been like before, how we had interacted, how he had seen me and I him.

Those months, war was everywhere: actively or brimming just below the surface.

He moved from place to place with ease, awake in one country and asleep in another. He was kind to everyone. He loved his home but understood the porosity of borders: of body, of story, of place, of time. He also understood their violence. He'd lived through war and recognized that the line between life and death was not as rigid as we might think; he'd lived through war and could not stomach ethno-nationalism of any kind, anything that might tinge of genocide or the breach of human rights. He believed in civic responsibility, a cultural tie, and was adamant that this was not the same as nationalism. I don't have a responsibility to nation, he always said. But I do to ghosts.

So, that was Luka. Though he was not without moments of torment, overall his disposition was bright-eyed and open. Little upset him in everyday life but much upset him in the world. His loneliness, if he felt it, did not impose obligation on others.

I was not overwhelmed by his need, because his need—those rare moments he showed it—seemed divorced from power or manipulation. His affection was warm and never smothering.

But when I was with Luka in particular, I often thought of the American woman who disappeared near the waterfalls, and sometimes late at night I felt a closeness with her, I became her, I'd have to wake and wash my face to tell myself I was not she. What was more was that sometimes I would recall something that I was sure had happened to me, and as I'd tell the story and hear it emerging in my own voice, I'd think, No, no, that was not me at all. Was it? A beloved, a roommate, a friend from my youth, our stories all merging and carrying over, a chorus of voices merging like dancers in a dance.

I am trying to impose a linearity on an experience that felt recursive, or even fractal: weeks nestled within weeks, stories within stories, bodies within bodies, words within words.

CLOSE TO THE END OF MY STAY AT THE TRANSLATION CENter, my French tenants called to say they were planning to return to France the following month. Their parents were aging and needed more help and they could no longer justify living so far away. They didn't know when they would return to Greece but hoped I'd consider letting them rent for shorter periods here and there.

We never meant to stay five years, they said, but they were grateful they could, and did.

And I said we'd work something out, not to worry.

So the house would soon be empty again.

I wanted to tell Luka about it, but something made me hesitate.

AT OUR TRANSLATORS' GOODBYE DINNER, WE DRANK A LOT of wine, and rakija, and then we sang karaoke at a pizza place atop a grocery store. The balcony was strewn with colored lights, and when the singing began, a disco ball glittered like a kaleidoscope. It was near an abandoned lot that seemed to be buzzing, and the bartender told us it was the grasshoppers. We drank beers and sang and each time we'd quiet down we heard them again.

This was not in the old town, which was used to noise, but in a neighborhood outside it. At eleven they had to turn things down, as the neighborhood was residential, and we ordered some pizza, a late-night snack. Our waiter was very tall and smiley and said that these were his favorite nights here: with the grasshoppers and not too many tourists, who would begin arriving in the middle of the month.

We walked back home in a pack, arms around one another like drunks in a cartoon. Marta and a few others promised to stay in touch, and Alexandra and Ioanna and I planned to meet when all back in Greece. The younger translators were crying, they'd never had such an experience before, and I could see it had been very moving to them. We grew quiet as we walked. I understood their sadness.

I had made no plans. Maybe I'd live in the house, which would soon be vacant. Maybe I'd go back to Athens, which is where Ioanna and Alexandra assumed they'd find me. But I wasn't ready to leave at all.

The moon was bright, and one owl called out, sounding both plaintive and proud.

WITHOUT MUCH DIFFICULTY, I RENTED A SMALL STUDIO A twenty-minute walk from the translators' center, not far from the pizza place. Marta knew the owners, distant friends of her parents', a woman named Lyuba, whose eighty-something mother, Neda, lived in the flat below me.

Lyuba said she would rent to me because I was one of theirs, and her mother lived downstairs and she wanted someone she could trust. That's how she said it, "one of ours," just like the grandmother of my childhood friend. She assumed, maybe because of Marta, that I was a diaspora return, who'd lost some of the language, someone who'd left as a child and now had come back—which, of course, was not without its complications. That was that.

There was no rental contract, no written agreement, and she didn't ask for my passport or any identifying information, which was surprising, considering the Balkan love of the paper-state, but also, I suppose, its resistance to it. Lyuba did not want to upset Neda with short-term renters. And she grimaced as she said that phrase, adding, They rent this shabby apartment and are upset when it's not a five-star hotel. I wouldn't have called it shabby, but eclectic. Its cramped yellow kitchen, brightly colored rugs, a comfortable red couch. I thought it suited me.

So the only thing of myself I had given her was an envelope of cash, and we sat at the small table outside the bakery across the street from the apartment and had a coffee and little cookies shaped like ravioli. I don't think she even knew my last name. She didn't ask many questions, so I remained a foreigner regardless, and surely she heard my accent, my mistakes. Or maybe all this made me belong. I am not sure.

In fact, at some point, I think I had planned to stay; normally as I near the end of a trip I start getting rid of things, giving away books and clothes I don't want to drag along. But instead I had begun to accumulate things: clothes and notebooks, a coffeemaker, kitchen implements, spices, books.

In that apartment I slept such a heavy, blank sleep that I awoke many mornings disoriented, my eyes blinking open at first light, and for a few seconds each morning I forgot where I was. I did not have nightmares; I was no longer always thinking of violence. I was happy. As if each morning I began again. For the first time in a decade I had no insomnia. I fell asleep when my head hit the pillow and woke just before the morning filtered in. I swam each sunrise.

So for a while I became someone who talked to strangers and stood in circles at parties, telling stories, engaged in banter, unashamed of my awkward syntax or slightly strange diction or my accent that was not rooted in place but instead inside the mix of other tongues I knew. No matter. The language, which I'd attempted to learn those years before, came back to me, and I settled into it. In fact, despite small mistakes here and there, I would say I spoke not with sophistication but at least with clarity. The words carried no emotional weight but the cadence and sounds did, and this gave me a particular ease, an imagined fluency before I was fluent.

Though it would seem that I would have felt transient there, I didn't; or I took the transience as a sort of state of being, not an in-between but a fact of the moment. I did not, as I might in other short-term situations, keep my eye on the calendar, subconsciously counting down days.

Maybe it was why I felt so comfortable. The fleetingness was its own feeling, and language gave the illusion of permanence. Strangers often didn't realize I was a foreigner until I stumbled over a basic word I had not yet learned: "blanket," "sidewalk," "saucepan." And I was not always aware of my errors, and this gave me a stupid freedom. So if you might wonder how I allowed this to happen, it was a liberation from the confines of selfhood and the exhausting language around it. The language of the self had gotten it all wrong, and I know I was part of that error.

I still read the news, read all the papers. I had for years been slipping away from social media anyway, but I deleted what remained of my accounts.

I began to enjoy a life that had little to do with what I broadcast, nearly shocked at the relief, that I had spent so many years living this way.

My first conversation with Neda was quick, and happened one morning after my swim. I returned home with my wet hair to find her waiting at the top of the stairs, outside her door. The sea had been so still that morning, and I'd swum for at least an hour. My swimming twin was there too, she almost always was, and she swam a long time too. We rarely talked at all, always a greeting, a wave goodbye.

Your hair, Neda said, reaching her hand out to touch it.

My wet hair upset her, she said it was too early in the season to swim, and I promised her I'd dry it right away. But you walked home like this, she said. It's too late.

It's too late, I echoed, nodding. In fairness to her, the morning was unusually chilly; I'd passed people wearing down vests over their T-shirts. Luka, too, said he rarely swam before July, and it was only the first week in June.

Yet there was such gravity in her voice that I had to hide my laughter. June was, to me, deep into summer, even though technically, I supposed, it was still spring.

I ENJOYED LIVING IN THAT SUN-DRENCHED OLD TOWN, the ancient stone streets, the old palace, the boardwalk where people paraded in the evening, dressed like stars, or sometimes like yoga enthusiasts. The summer season began and the population doubled, at least, yet this transience and constant movement calmed me in a way that surprised me. Luka pointed out that once July came, I'd feel differently. Fair enough.

To live alone in a place like this was far different from living together with a bunch of people, as I had at the translation center; in some ways, it felt like a new town entirely. Time stretched out in front of me. I recognized faces. Who would know me, whom would I know, did anyone recognize me? I took long walks alone on the path along the sea. Sometimes I walked past a massive hotel resort that looked like an old, communist wonderland, and I imagined at one point it had its charms.

I worked in the early mornings until midafternoon. Mostly I saw Luka in the evenings.

Though he was often away, moving between this island and the coast, his permanent home where his son, in his early twenties, now lived. His son, he said, was happy to have the place for himself and his girlfriend, and Luka said he was happy to stay here, in that small apartment. I didn't know if he owned it or rented and I didn't ask.

He did not wait for me, or make himself available in a passive-aggressive way, something that for reasons hard to pinpoint always gave me great stress, to always be the one to initiate something because the other person was always waiting.

Luka lived on the opposite side of the port, so that the busy port and its old town were a meeting place for us, and when we drove from my house to his we took the road that ran on the town's periphery. But when I walked there I went along the sea, so in a way, some days, I'd encircle the town entirely.

I saw him when I saw him and didn't when I didn't and this all felt perfect to me, not to feel obligated to check in, and even though I knew my time with him was limited, there was never a feeling of duty. He often spent days working on something, night shifting into morning into afternoon, and sometimes he wouldn't recall if we'd seen each other that morning or two mornings before. He had traveled a lot, often to war zones, and he said the things he saw would never leave him. His heart was always broken. But we had little need for backstory, talked little of our pasts or our separate presents, and he never assumed I did something the way I did something because of any sort of ethnic identity; besides, our cultures were similar enough, though I knew it was often similarity, not difference, that bred contempt. He, too, had parents of different ethnicities, and we both hated the idea of any sort of purity, or pureness. Despite his comment years ago about my Americanness, this rarely came up. We knew enough not to ascribe any one trait to any one self and instead understood each other as composites.

I suppose I'd say we were seeing each other, though even that doesn't quite describe it. No matter. For a while, I settled happily into this new life that had been written for me. This life, this name.

But war raged, both far away and close, one war in particular my maternal grandparents had predicted would come since I was a child. I was glad they were no longer alive to see it. When that war became more real across the world, at least for a while, hearing the national anthem I had memorized as a child, one of my first songs, could still brought me to tears.

I'd always been a news addict, reading in the morning and the evening and sometimes in the middle of the night. Luka could not watch the news on television, he said—even though he, as a journalist, often appeared on television himself—but when I was alone, I tuned in. On the weekends Luka bought several papers, the only way to approach something like fact, he said, and read them all, all day. Sometimes, Luka read things to me. I began to sink into novels, which was where all the truth was anyway, from where so much of my political consciousness was shaped.

Every so often I'd feel the deep awareness of another reality folding out before me, a subterranean stream, echoes of echoes, but mostly I accepted things for what they were.

WHERE IS YOUR HOME? NEDA ASKED ME ONE MORNING. I told her I lived in the flat above her, that we were neighbors, and she said, No, no, your origins. I told her, and also about my father's Greek house by the sea, the river and waterfalls not far from there that shared her name. One of the only Greek rivers with a feminine name.

She stared at me a long time, and then asked if I'd help her down the stairs.

Lyuba appeared at the door and said, Mama, I'll take you down.

Neda's question felt like a portal that would suck me back to another life.

All the rivers here are feminine, she said, and then laughed, incredulous at my apparent foolishness.

I'D READ ABOUT THIS ISLAND'S ANCIENT, UNDERGROUND rivers, its sunken stone road, the submerged walls in the sea. Several years before this, I'd watched a documentary about the ancient underground rivers of Athens, and ever since, I had been unable to walk through the neighborhood behind the ancient stadium without wondering what ran beneath my feet. And somewhere else I'd read that those who grew up swimming in rivers can feel those rivers in the sea when they swim.

THAT ENCOUNTER WITH THE FERRYMAN, AS I BEGAN TO think of him, remained in my mind as a composite sketch of all my disconcerting involvements—as if life offered us these summations—with the undertone of violence that I had learned to detect since I was a child. Every so often a menacing feeling returned, sometimes like the barely detectable rumbles of a small earthquake, other times a weight on my chest, or a strange pit in my stomach, an emotion that despite my access to several languages, or perhaps because of it, I could not quite name. But it was residual, I think, something I carried around with me.

But I want to be clear: This was no Calypso situation. I was not forced to stay, and I did not sit sobbing on the shores of the fruitless sea, dreaming of hearth smoke. Later, I would hope for a boat, though not for escape. Besides, I'd never quite believed Calypso imprisoned Odysseus exactly. He was skilled in many ways, after all. I'm sure he could have figured something out.

ONE MORNING, WHILE WE WERE SITTING IN A CAFÉ NEAR his apartment, Luka asked if I wanted to stay here while he was gone. I did not want him to live with me and he did not seem to want me to live with him, though we never mentioned this directly. I thought it was understood between us, the way many things were understood.

What do you mean by "stay"? I asked. I wasn't even sure where he was headed next.

Because I thought at first he meant in his flat, which did not make sense, unless he was asking me to give up my flat. Then I thought he meant this country. I had not come here for him, though maybe I had stayed for him. I wasn't sure why I had stayed. I could not detect the meaning underneath the question: Was he asking my general plans, or did he feel he had some control in my decision?

Here, he said, gesturing to the café where we sat, where we often came, but meaning, in his place. So you don't have to pay rent.

Thank you, I said. That's very generous. But no need.

His place, on a narrow street away from the touristy area, was writerly but not stuffy, clean and airy but cozy, with a sprawling desk that overlooked the street and had its back to the large open kitchen, the view of the pale hills in the distance. Besides the stack of books on the coffee table and those little notebooks he seemed to keep in every pocket, his special pencils, there was no clutter. It's not that he didn't have things, he did; everything just had its own place. Once in a while, several coffee cups were stacked on his desk. His various electronics were always in their place, whereas I had a tangle of chargers and adapters and plugs that I could never find. He had four coffee mugs, four plates, four water glasses, four wine. A smattering of glasses for whiskey and beer and clothes that could be packed in one small suitcase. The couch was huge and soft and gray. There was a flokati rug he'd bought in Athens. He claimed I had been with him, but I think I only told him where to go to buy it. He insisted I'd haggled with the guy, that the shop owner had flirted with me. Could be.

Had we been together then, shopping in Athens? Even when I met him so many years ago it seemed he was an old friend, an olive tree with deep roots. Luka's friendship felt like a constant even though it was far from it. There were long periods of time, months, years, when we didn't talk at all. One of the few friendships that did not fade without constant communication, and more to do with a sense of being.

He was going back to the mainland, he said. Family party. His son had gotten engaged and he wanted to celebrate with them.

I can water your plants for you, if you like, I said. I often did this when he was gone. He had three plants he loved and a bunch of herbs and ferns on the balcony.

But this was also my way of saying, I understand that I'm not invited, don't worry, please go have a fun time. We talked so little of the future, it was as though it didn't exist. Sometimes, he'd look at me, deep in thought, and I wondered exactly what—and whom—he saw.

I imagine he knew I'd return to Greece soon, but it never crossed my mind to ask him to come along. Maybe he was waiting for an invitation. He had traveled a lot, mostly for work, but this country was his home. He felt a deep obligation to it, felt tethered to its landscape, whereas I floated across the waves.

LATER THAT DAY, LUKA DID A NEWS SPOT LIVE FROM THE table on my balcony—he liked the light—wearing a pressed blue oxford and his sweatpants. I sat inside, watching him on the television. There was such a levity to him, despite the sorts of things he was reporting, and these were things we often talked about late at night: child trafficking rings, unaccompanied minors disappearing in western Europe, his overwhelm at wanting to talk about things the world did not want him to talk about. The way there was never an agent, only passive voice: A village was bombed, a five-year-old boy was hit by a stray bullet. We talked about the tension that came from standing apart while something horrific unfolded, and how one time, after interviewing a young refugee couple, he'd given them one hundred euros from his wallet, knowing it defied the ethics of his profession but not of his life.

I don't know how to write about all this, he said.

Is that a line from your novel? I asked, and as I said it my voice felt strange. I became aware of its reverberations, my voice leaving my body.

The novel, he said. He looked uncomfortable and then laughed.

It all goes in, right? I said. We have to write about these things.

He didn't talk to me about his novel. It existed in another space, even though I apparently wandered around it. Most translators would agree that each new translation affects the first version, the first original. I kept mulling that around in my mind, wondering what it meant to translate a real person into a story, and how the original was forever changed.

But I didn't say any of this to Luka. Instead, I told him about two Greek poems. The first, by Nikos Engonopoulos, asks how we can write poetry in times of strife; it's as though we write on the backs of death announcements. And another poet, Manolis Anagnostakis, replied to him with a poem of his own, noting the unanswered sobs of a child, tattered flags with holes, nightmares. And my favorite, the chilling way the poem ends with a parenthetical: "(But who will speak with pain of all this?)"

He thought about this, asked me to find him the poems. Then I heard him open my refrigerator, move things around, looking for something. You never have any milk, he said.

It's a big commitment, I said, and he laughed, though weakly.

Are you sure this isn't too much of a commitment? he said, dropping his set of keys into an empty kitchen drawer.

Your plants? I think I can manage.

He laughed once more, though I'm not sure why.

THE NEXT MORNING I WOKE TO LUKA HOVERING OVER ME.
You were barely breathing, it scared me, he said.

I'd had another blank, dreamless sleep and felt an odd heaviness in my limbs. For a few moments I was unable to move my body. Yet I did not feel afraid, I felt light, as if while I slept I'd solved something, or left something heavy behind.

Don't be scared, I said. Luka always acted as though I were about to disappear, to the point that I wondered if I was disappearing already. Not in a needy way, as if he were afraid of abandonment—though I understood that feeling too. It was more matter-of-fact, like he knew there was an expiration date. But of course the things we fear in others are the things we recognize in ourselves, and I understand now that Luka was not afraid of my disappearance as much as his own impermanence.

And it was his place, not mine, that had the feeling of temporariness. Mine, in contrast, felt like I'd been living there forever. How did I get so many piles of paper, so many scraps of things? Had I traveled with all those shoes, now piled by the door, and the stack of books on my nightstand?

I was drinking a coffee and dressing to swim and telling Luka, still in bed, about the conversation I'd had weeks earlier with the woman about the jellyfish. He got out of bed and began to dress to accompany me to the beach. Luka never came with me in the morning. For one, the water was still too cold—it was fine—and he knew it was a quiet morning ritual for me. If he woke with me he usually dashed off for a run.

I don't think you need to come, in case I get stung, I said. I swim every day just fine.

But he said, No, no, I'm not worried about the jellyfish. I've been stung many times. I feel like a walk.

We arrived earlier than usual; Luka's prompting had gotten me out an hour before and the sun was still rising.

The sea was glorious that morning, the water luscious. I melted into it.

Nothing makes me feel more like part of the natural world, the more-than-human natural world, than swimming in the sea at sunrise, the light coming in and my swimming through it, particularly those long swims, like when I'd swim out to the far rock, or an open-water swimming event I'd done in the Sporadic islands several years before. The feeling of being not an observer but an inhabitant or, more clearly, that the sea also inhabits me. I am not a visitor, though maybe, I hope, a gentle guest. Moving through what was here before, to those thermal vents in the sea from which all life sprung.

Along the rocky perimeter of the cove I saw the young octopus again, watching me before dashing away. A completely unnerving feeling, to be seen like that. Was it the same one? I like to think it was, the strange recognition it gave me: Oh, you again, hello, hope you figure things out. I'd seen the film about the diver who befriends an octopus and had been undone by it. I swam a little while and saw him again, this time near a copse of sea anemones.

When I exited the water I didn't see Luka and I felt a twinge, the tightness in my chest I recognized as uncertainty, followed by an eerie calm that says, Okay, we cannot know or understand everything. The feeling of reaching the end of the book and wondering where the story would stop and also feeling as though it continued, somewhere, without me.

I had forgotten my towel and dried off in the sun, stripping my suit off underneath my hoodie, noticing how thin and faded and stretched out it had become, how all my swimsuits had become. Sometimes when I swam I'd find myself holding my bottoms up with one hand. I'd buy some new ones. An early swim with the morning air still a bit cool, the emergence from the water into warm dry clothes and the sun; my god, it was a kind of perfection. I closed my eyes and listened to the gulls, one lonely cicada, the floisvos of the waves. I was thirsty but had also forgotten my water bottle.

I could feel the space shift and when I opened my eyes there was Luka, walking toward me, holding a towel. Had he brought that with him? The only disagreements we had were about being cold, catching cold, the inherent danger of a cross-breeze on one's neck; the worst thing you could do in his apartment was open up windows in the front and the back and let the breeze go surging through, a fear that seemed to preoccupy much of southeast Europe. Forget about putting ice in your drink. Sometimes Luka's folk superstitions, which I found endearing, felt like those of a prior generation or two. Then again, so did mine.

I stood to greet him. Though I'd already dressed, Luka playfully wrapped the towel around me.

Then he whispered something in my ear but I could not make it out, I could not hear where the words stopped and ended or what language they were in, if any language at all.

We walked back to my place.

THAT NIGHT, I WOKE WITH NIGHTMARES. I MUST HAVE cried out and woken Luka because he quietly put his arm on my shoulder and said I was okay. He said he used to have terrible nightmares, sometimes still did, and sometimes it helped to say them out loud, to release them. But I couldn't remember anything but a feeling of dread. If men create violence, and the rest of us store it in our bodies, how do we translate it? It was a half-formed thought, but it kept repeating in my half-awake mind.

And then I said it: How do we translate violence?

What do you mean? he asked. He was up now, heating the water in the kettle, making chamomile.

Into language, you mean?

I don't know, I said. Then I told him about the man on the ferry.

Luka did not seem alarmed by this at all but listened. I have never known someone to listen so well, and maybe this was all in the pages of his novel, the novel that was me and not me.

He said: You can feel threatened even if there is no threat.

Could be, I said. But are you writing it as it happens?

I'm not following, he said.

I told him I had always had a feeling of unease before something bad happened.

Like your grandmother, he said.

I've told you about that?

Yeah, he said. When you told me about the carjacking. My mother was the same.

Right, I said. That I did remember.

America is a very violent place. He said it as half question, half declaration.

Yeah, I said. Violence was everywhere, or maybe I had become more attuned to it. Not to even mention the persistent violence of empire, of aggression, of a want to possess. Or perhaps I do mean these things but on a smaller scale. It wasn't that I had not been prey to it; it was that its slow accretion made me inured to its violations.

The city I had lived in for many years was often talked about in terms of its ruin and its danger, and like all cities it had its challenges. Though it was a lively and wonderful city and I'd never, before the carjacking, been a victim of crime there, in the city limits. Not to say it didn't exist, of course. It did.

And more moments, those lodged in my memory, emerged as I continued to talk. When I was seven, I overheard a family friend tell the story of her husband's rage, and the image, from her description, of the way he shoved her hand in the garbage disposal and threatened to turn it on, has never left me. I still have that nightmare. I am still afraid of the garbage disposal, and from a young age I learned to fear not men but their rage and often compromised myself to avoid it.

When I began to list the instances of violence and violation I myself had experienced, I knew that they were the instances of probably any woman my age. Not to say they were mild. There'd been an older neighborhood boy when I was just a kid and, years later, my chemistry lab partner. There had been all those yeses that should have been nos and maybe were inside me, struggling to get out—or maybe they were nos that were not heard at all. And then the countless unwanted pats in the bars where I waited tables. I'd been groped on a plane from Paris to New York, and on a plane from Chicago to Amsterdam, a man masturbated next to me and I, somehow, was too shocked to move until he got up to use the bathroom and I asked the flight attendant if I could change my seat. She didn't ask for a reason.

Ask women about their experiences on planes and you will be shocked, I said to Luka.

I'm sorry, he said. He placed a mug of tea in front of me and sat down with his own.

I closed my eyes. Thank you, I said.

Are you sure you're okay?

I'm okay, I said.

He was quiet, but in my mind the list continued: In the graduate library in Ann Arbor, I'd hid in a closed study carrel for two hours while an active shooter ran loose. I had been robbed twice at gunpoint: once at the small bakery in my college town, and once at an ice cream shop where I worked in high school, in a suburban strip mall where much of my neighborhood went in the evenings. I'd witnessed a robbery at the bank in the suburb my family had moved to right before my parents got divorced. I'd been in my school uniform, cashing my ice cream check, and the man had come in, shouted for us to get on the floor, and jumped over the teller window where I had been standing. When I narrate all these things at once, they seem, to me, self-absorbed and insignificant. I had never expressed all these things as a list before. They were simply things that happened. To return to them, moments I had until now long forgotten, felt solipsistic.

Mostly, though, my memory has jumbled these instances, the way a cable television channel you did not subscribe to looked when you switched to it—a detail of my youth I remember only now, in the telling. Memory is amorphous, but the act of remembering takes on a form. Remembering naturally groups things, aligns things, makes connections. I was recognizing and I was voicing, and as Sontag wrote of remembering, it all seemed a form of address.

I didn't know exactly what this disquiet was. It was not menace, nor was it uneasiness. I wanted to sit with it.

THOUGH I'VE ALWAYS BEEN VERY INDEPENDENT, A TRAIT some might say has more to do with necessity than with courage, saying goodbye to Luka when he left to see his son felt more fraught this time around. He had come and gone before and I hadn't given it much thought. I suppose because he was going home, and this served as a reminder I was not a part of that life. No matter. Yet with Luka gone, I kept asking myself who I was in this place.

But I was here, with or without him, and I was antsy to work. A certain problem of syntax and meaning I'd untangled in my sleep and I wanted to return to it before I lost it, like it was passing through me and I myself could inadvertently destroy it, could dampen its light.

Voice, for me, was the hardest thing to re-create: the sensibility, as though it were not part of the text but floated symbiotically above it, and I was required to translate both streams. Sometimes it felt as though voice bodied through me, a three-dimensional thing of both language and its shadow. Other times it felt as though I thrashed between the lines of text, coughing, water lapping into my mouth, catching my arm on a word, a phrase.

There was something this time around, of not knowing where the story was heading—an unknowing that applied to more than the story alone—that made the translation feel flickering and alive.

I WAS DRINKING AN AFTERNOON COFFEE AROUND THE corner from my apartment, and from my favorite table I could see the front door of my building. Luka was still out of town and I enjoyed the prospect of the days ahead of me, the translation unfolding along with them.

That afternoon, there was a chill to the breeze, but the sun was warm on my face, my body comfortable in a T-shirt and jeans. A handsome man in sunglasses and a beard, slightly older than Luka, in his fifties, nodded at me from the other side of the café. The sun was in my eyes, though, so I could not recognize him. He could have been anyone.

The door to my building flung open and stayed like that awhile, as if something were holding it open. But from where I sat, I couldn't see. Every few seconds I could see it wobble, as if about to close, as if whatever was holding it was not strong enough. Then Neda's walker emerged and, finally, Neda.

Neda looked both ways into the narrow street, up toward the café where I sat, and the other way, toward the road that led to the sea. The expression on her face—triumphant—suggested she might make a break and run, but the flight of stairs had surely taken away her strength, and instead she rested on the stone bench by the door. Across from the bench was an assortment of potted plants: tomatoes and herbs and flowers too.

She rooted around in a large bucket beneath the bench, where there was a hose coiled up. I'd seen Lyuba use it to wash down the street. There were street sweepers too, but what can I say, she liked a clean pathway. Neda wrestled it from the bucket, unwinding it, and tested the nozzle, which sprayed a steady stream into the road. She settled in on the bench and used it to spray the plants, several steps away. The joy in her face!

Down the street, I saw Lyuba walking toward the building, glancing at her phone. When she saw Neda outside, she broke into a trot. Mama, she yelled. What is going on? But Neda kept watering until she seemed satisfied and then, for good measure, washed the entryway of the building next door.

Neda and Lyuba saw me coming and Neda eyed me with curiosity, as she often did, as though we'd known each other long ago, in another life. You should watch out, she said. She waved her hand but trailed off.

I paused and waited, wasn't sure what she was referring to.

Watch out, she continued, or I'll steal your husband.

At first I thought I had misunderstood, but when it registered, I laughed, and then Lyuba laughed, and then Neda laughed the loudest of all, all three of us standing in a triangle. Neda sprayed her hose again and then slumped over. This had been a lot of activity for the day, I supposed, and suddenly she seemed ready to rest. She gave the plants one more spritz.

I'll help you back up, Mama, Lyuba said. The building had three stories, and I was glad Neda lived only one flight up. Please don't go down the stairs without me.

To observe the tenderness and exasperation that passed between them felt so intimate I thought I knew them myself, so I assumed a too-informal casualness with them, which I realize they might have simply attributed to my foreignness. I could hear them come and go in the echo of the stairwell, some days, though other days passed and I heard not a thing.

Neda's chatter was reassuring; it filtered in through my kitchen window. She talked about people as if they'd been over the day before when I could sense, somehow, that they'd been gone a very long time. She was worrying about the water. Did you go to the well, she'd ask Lyuba, and Lyuba would tell her yes, of course, she had fetched the water that morning.

WHEN LUKA RETURNED, HE CAME OVER, AND I HEARD Neda flirting with him in the stairwell, outside her door, and then I heard two sets of feet coming up the stairs. He came inside, gave me a kiss, and took a beer from the fridge. Neda waited at the door. I watched him give it to her, and her face lit up.

She asked me to open it and she beamed as I used the opener on my key chain, emblazoned with the word PHAROS, which meant "lighthouse" and was also the name of a beloved taverna in my dad's town. But it was also the ancient city and archaeological site not far from here, which Luka and I had visited, and which was named after the island of Paros, whose citizens had colonized this place. The way Neda looked at me was unnerving, as if she saw something astounding in me that I could not see.

I invited her to sit at the table, but she was already out the door, slowly going back down the stairs with the beer. She called to Luka, Congratulations to your son.

Later that evening, Lyuba knocked and asked if I had given Neda something to drink, and I said, Yes, it's possible, and she said, Please don't do that, and disappeared back into her mother's apartment, where Neda was singing a song like she was atop a mountain.

LUKA INVITED ME TO ACCOMPANY HIM ON A WEEKEND visit to Ivan's place on the mainland. The car ferries only departed from the port thirty minutes away, so on a gloriously bright Friday, we took those winding roads to the island's other side, where I'd been only once before, when Luka and I had walked through the olive groves those first days at the translation center. We'd taken a boat, so I'd experienced the landscape from the sea.

The ride was winding and pretty, and as we left the borders of the more carefully curated tourist town, the landscape was punctuated with the mundane—old trucks, laundry on the lines, groves of olive trees, a house where a woman tended to her flowers while a group of older men played cards. And as we left the outskirts of the town, we passed through a valley filled with old stoves and refrigerators, and hills whose origins from the seafloor you could see, the vertical push of shifting tectonic plates. Despite the busy-town feel of the port town where we stayed, the island seemed otherwise sparsely inhabited. Every so often, from a turn in the road, you might see a smattering of houses up a hill, but otherwise it was just cliffs and the sea.

Driving through that limestone and dolomite, the dramatic vertical peaks of it, I saw the power of currents, of ancient rivers. Water wants to go where it once was, dissolving minerals and seeping into stone, creating systems of subterranean streams and caves, caves high up in the hills.

When we drove through a dark tunnel carved right into the mountain, it seemed we would never come out. I had driven through mountain tunnels before, but never this long, never without sensing the light on the other side. The tunnel went on and on. As we moved through the earth into darkness, only one car's length ahead of us visible, I could sense Luka's body tense up, as if he were holding his breath. When the end of the tunnel was visible, he exhaled loudly, yet when we emerged from the tunnel he pulled over to the side of the road and got out. I waited in the passenger seat a moment, thinking he had to pee. After a minute I got out too, careful not to trample a patch of poppies on the side of the road. They dotted the landscape, and Luka stood among them, staring out at something. The old stone retaining walls carved the hillside like rivers.

Luka? I asked.

He turned to look at the road, as if a memory had surged up from it, pernicious and menacing.

Do you want to narrate or be narrated? he finally asked.

What?

Luka leaned on the car, stretching out his calves, the way he did before he ran in the mornings.

I did not understand why he was so rattled. Surely he'd known about this tunnel and had driven here often enough. Something about the tunnel? I asked.

Maybe, he said. He put his arms around me, his chin on my head, and didn't say anything else.

After a few minutes, he handed me his phone and said: Take my photo?

Sure, I said. The light was gorgeous and in his light green shirt against the muted brown-and-green backdrop, the poppies, the sea beyond the rocks, he looked handsome and melancholy, staring into the camera, relaxed and intense all at once. We took a few photos at several angles, a headshot, and from farther away. He looked beautiful and I felt a knot in my throat.

Without saying a word, we walked back to the car. Maybe you want to drive, he said. At least to the ferry.

This was his way of saying he did not want to drive.

The road from here is not too winding, he said.

So I said okay and drove us to the ferry and was reassured by how comfortable and capable I felt, despite the manual transmission. He relaxed.

I was struck by the way the town where I stayed, though charming, had a medieval feel juxtaposed with the placelessness of certain trends, cafés, the same touristy shops you find anywhere in the world. A shop of rubber ducks, for instance, which I'd also seen in Barcelona and maybe somewhere else too. And it was so clean. Pristine even, like a movie set—it did appear in many films, and those weeks I was there I often ran into film crews.

But on the other side of the tunnel, everything felt different to me, much more familiar than the more manicured section of town I'd been spending most of my time in. It reminded me of the outskirts of my father's birthplace, or an untouristy Greek island, or a small village in Bulgaria. Yet we were on the same island as always; we hadn't gone far at all. Borders were conceptual and shifting, and it was on that drive that I felt the contrived nature of where I stayed, the apartments where people lived like locals while the locals lived elsewhere.

And as I drove onto the ferry, I felt a sense of both past and premonition.

The ferry ride calmed Luka a bit, and when we walked back to the car before disembarking, he made no mention of not driving, as if I'd never taken the keys.

Along the coast, the drive was gorgeous. The hillside was occasionally dotted with houses, and Luka pointed out plants: lavender, agave, salt cedar trees.

Ivan's house was on its own tiny peninsula that jutted from the mainland, and Ivan insisted his guests park their cars and come across by boat, so we waited in a small gravel lot to be ferried across the channel. Surely Ivan was able to reach it by car; this seemed to be quite a power move, or a ridiculous one.

Luka noticed my bafflement.

Do you always arrive this way? I asked.

No. Sometimes. It's how he likes his guests to arrive. More grand.

What if we want to come and go? I asked.

From the small boat, as we turned into the cove, we saw Ivan's large, ochre-colored house looming in the distance, appearing like a mirage. Though Luka claimed Ivan said the road was narrow and he didn't want people's cars getting stuck, I was sure he had his guests arrive this way so they could see his house from the sea. Luka pointed out the small beach where we could swim, and the way you could scramble up a rocky path and enter Ivan's house from his wine cellar.

He has money like no one here has money, Luka finally said, I think partly for my benefit, to note that most of his friends were not like this.

Oh, not from publishing, he said when I asked. That's his hobby, just like his olive groves and fruit trees, the lavender, the brandy. He doesn't do it for the money but because he has money. His father died young, he went to London when we were in our twenties, his mother married a very rich man who had all sorts of ties with investors and developers, all that development on the coasts.

I didn't realize, I said. I thought of all those luxury hotels cropping up on cliffs over the Ionian and Aegean.

He spent a year diverting the stream so it ran right near his land.

What?

I'm serious, Luka said. He grew up near a river and really liked the sound of the stream rushing down the hill.

I recalled Marta saying something like this, that Ivan was a man who would change the course of a river. I had not taken it literally.

What Luka could never say out loud to me, but what I think was implied, was that he had to stay in Ivan's good graces. Was he some sort of benefactor, or did this go back to their youth? When Luka wanted me to know something, he offered. But this was the first time I detected a hint of judgment in his voice, or envy, as well as some reticence.

Ivan and I have been friends since childhood, he said. As if to indicate: But this is not my world.

I recalled, at the festival, him and Ivan getting into an argument about something. Ivan, I think as part of a power struggle with Luka, could be both deeply defensive of the country and highly condescending at once, and I could tell this bothered Luka, who was neither of these things. Luka was not always trying to be cosmopolitan, whatever that meant. I admired this about him: his complete dedication to a place, his acceptance of faults and difficult history and less-than-virtuous stories and his deep knowledge of pain.

We'll have fun though, Luka added.

I'll give him this: Ivan was a very generous host—though the sort of host who wanted you to see and comment on his generosity, whose hosting was a kind of sovereignty, to make clear where the power was.

IVAN AND A SPRITELIKE WOMAN CALLED LENA—WHITE-blond hair, pale skin, light eyes—greeted us at the door. I recalled her from the night of the play, performatively sullen at the end of the table and the palpable tension between her and Marta. Luka had mentioned that Ivan was with someone new, but I associated him so much with Marta that I had forgotten. I had the urge to text her, to tell her where I was, but even though I'd gleaned that she'd been the one to end it with Ivan, I knew something in the relationship had wounded her too. No need to stir things up for her.

Lena talked about Ivan as if he were the most brilliant man on earth, nearly gushing. She was talking about the watershed, his tricks of irrigation, as if Ivan had done it all himself with his own hands as opposed to a crew of guys he'd probably hired and paid nothing. I was surprised by this, that Lena would not challenge a guy like Ivan. I supposed she was in love with him, or maybe drawn to what she saw as power.

The water here is excellent, she continued. Ivan gets it from a stream. It's said to clear kidney stones, other ailments, a miracle water.

I had known men like Ivan all my life, if not wealthy like this then at least as arrogant; honestly, they amused me, their transparencies, their easily wounded egos, their need to mark their territory, to own, to provoke, to collect. I am sure Marta had seen something in him, his charm, his connections, his intense way of looking, or ignoring. But my experience of his intensity, the way he watched Marta from across the terrace, was more sinister, a proprietary, chilling gaze.

Lena then turned to me and began telling me about some

of the other guests who were coming for dinner—the neighbors who lived across the cove. British. A group of young American filmmakers Ivan had met at the minimarket; they were renting the small house up the road, and Ivan had a thing for inviting new people, particularly those he wanted to impress, or challenge. Luka told me that the coasts and islands were crawling with filmmakers now, something about tax breaks and low costs.

Every movie set in Greece or Italy is actually filmed here, Lena said.

I nodded, not knowing how she was hoping I'd respond. To whom was it supposed to be more offensive, that Greece and Italy were being dramatized in Croatia, or that Croatia had to pretend to be something it was not? Or maybe she was suggested something more simple: That to much of the world, these places were vacation places, the locals disappeared in favor of the vistas, the landscapes, the picturesque.

Lena hoped the filmmakers were not easily offended; they—we, Americans—were all so sensitive and politically correct, she said. I laughed—I'd heard this so many times that it was becoming tiresome, even irrelevant, everything else considered, but of course I knew what she meant—and told her I thought we'd survive. I realized she was trying to provoke me. Of course, though, she was right: Americans were quite good at performing their offended-ness, their political virtue, and as my Greek friends often noted, could never see things beyond our own narrow frame of reference.

We settled in.

Every detail was attended to: the linens, the extra little things in our own bathroom, the towels arranged just so, as well as a particular schedule of meals and drinks. I flopped onto the big bed, which rose from the floor like a mountain, positioned on a beautiful wooden platform, three steps above the floor. A bed made of wood from the olive trees. Luka followed, kissing me and then rolling onto his back to look at the ceiling. The setting sun angled in through the windows, making a patch of warmth on the bed. Luka was tired, the drive seemed to have exhausted him, but Ivan had a schedule for the evening and drinks were supposed to be at seven.

This place is drenched with sunlight, Luka said, yet he refuses to install solar panels.

Doesn't seem like the kind of guy worried about the expense.

He doesn't like the way they look, Luka said, and shrugged playfully.

This place feels like some surreal hotel, I said.

Luka laughed.

This is going to be a very strange weekend, I said, isn't it.

AT DINNER—PROMPTLY AT EIGHT—I SAT NEXT TO THE British couple who owned a house across the small cove. We could see it from the terrace. They were very nice, albeit a bit professorial, and I had the feeling, as the evening went on, that I should have crammed for the exam. There was no ancient cave or tree, no stone or ruin, no epic or myth, that these two could not lecture about. Charming, maybe, but a type; they could not celebrate an ancient glory without maligning a place's contemporary dwellers. See the Victorians.

They were sweet enough, though, and were talking about a cruise they'd just taken, based on *The Odyssey*.

Oh, it was great fun, they said. We are not cruise people, Kathryn added.

Yes, it was a whim, Philip said. A friend of ours was lecturing.

Kathryn turned to me. How did you come to translation?

And I told them part of the truth: a class in translation when I was a graduate student.

Ancient Greek? Philip asked, or really, he stated.

No, I said.

When I was a graduate student, we had a language requirement. It was assumed that most admitted students would already have knowledge of a foreign language, so we could easily test out of this requirement if we wanted. I could have done so in French, which I'd studied for years. I was not raised speaking Greek, I learned that later, but Ukrainian, my mother's language. Part of my excitement about the university was its Modern Greek studies program, where I could finally formally study the language I had stumbled through on visits back to Greece each summer.

If I'd wanted to study Ancient Greek, or take the Ancient Greek exam for that matter, this would have been fine with my department. But I'd genuinely wanted to study Modern Greek.

But this is what upset me: The chair of my department, a man much like Philip, smugly told me that Modern Greek was not considered a language with a potential for translation. (No matter that Cavafy's "The First Step" had been printed on our welcome materials.) A language that had produced two Nobel Prize winners was not, somehow, considered a language of literature. It was relegated to the local, the kitsch, the language spoken in the kitchens of restaurants and in the basements of Greek Orthodox churches. And therefore, not a scholarly language. A language without universal appeal.

But I didn't say any of this. No, no, not Ancient. Modern Greek.

So your roots are in Greece, Kathryn said.

Some of them. But then I added: What is it Gertrude Stein said? What good are roots if you can't take them with you?

They laughed.

During a lull in the conversation, everyone turned to Luka's conversation with the American filmmakers. Two of them were asking him about what it was like to have lived through those wars. How in the world did they expect anyone to answer that? Luka was quiet, and then he excused himself.

Ivan said, in a strange, lighthearted voice: Well, it was pretty terrible! Lena said: I'm going to change the music, any requests? And I liked them both then. Kathryn was asking me about my translation, mentioning how Philip only read when he could read in the original language, but she mostly read work in translation. I told her about the book I was finishing and she wrote the author's name down, and the title.

When Lena returned, one of the Americans asked her about her work, if it had been translated into English.

Lena said that it had.

Dozens of languages, added Ivan.

Luka returned to the table. When I caught his eye he smiled and took a drink.

Oh, that's wonderful, Kathryn said.

I suppose. I found the whole experience traumatic, Lena said.

Traumatic? Philip said, laughing, though I'm not sure at what, as he didn't believe in translation at all.

He thought she was joking, or at least being self-deprecating, but Lena did not have access to self-deprecation. She wasn't particularly witty or warm or funny. I don't think I ever saw her smile. She was pretty dismissive from the moment we arrived.

This was not a new attitude, necessarily; one of my favorite translators, who worked from Turkish to English, no longer translated the work of the writer with whom I associated her. I heard that they'd had a falling out, that she was ruining his work. Yet this seemed to me as much about personal complexities between them as anything else. Then again, what was more personal than one's writing?

Lena's face grew red. I realize it's a privilege to be translated like this, she said, looking first at me and then around the table. But the experience was violent. She took a cigarette from her bag and held it in her hand. Then she placed it on the table.

Violent? I said, wondering if she'd misspoken. Not even "violating." And then I didn't know what to say, so I said I was sorry she'd had a bad experience.

It wasn't one experience. It's the whole idea. I mean, these are my words, my story! Why should I have to give up control of it!

Do you? I asked. Have to?

Why do you agree? asked Luka. Why not simply say no? I recognized the look on his face, the same as when he'd asked me, Who are you to write about this? His face and neck were flushed.

Lena looked at us both as though we were idiots but said nothing.

Despite any good will he might have felt for her when she graciously changed the subject, Luka now remained agitated. I think it was Lena's mention of violence. He hated that every uncomfortable or unfortunate thing was now called a trauma.

He continued: Why not allow something else then to be translated instead of taking up a translator's time? I would love to be translated the way you are, he added, and I knew he'd immediately regret it.

Look, she said. My language is a small one.

So is mine, Luka said.

If I wrote in English I'd have an entirely different career. A house like this, a different life. And then she looked at Luka, intimately. Maybe you would too.

I was surprised by this level of assuredness. From what I understood, her books did well in many languages. Lena went on about several other writers that she considered her peers, how she felt her writing was so much better than all of it.

Kathryn turned to me, bored of the conversation, as though changing a television channel. We've been to Greece many times, she said. We love it. We were torn, where to buy. It's far less chaotic here, Philip added.

It is lovely here, I said, though I was trying to follow Luka's conversation with Ivan and Lena. The British writer's name came up and Ivan scoffed and he and Lena exchanged a glance. She rolled her eyes.

Sure, Kathryn said, turning back to me. It's beautiful, and one of the less sad places. I don't really care for these surrounding Balkans. It's not really Europe, is it?

Well, it is, I said, but I didn't feel like getting into it. I had heard this type of condescension toward Greece as well: it was everywhere during the years of the global financial crisis. Her dismissal of such a large and complex region where they had chosen to buy a house was not uncommon, nor was the idea that southeast Europe wasn't really Europe. Less sad places? It wasn't as though the UK had a reputation for its cheerfulness, or a tradition that lacked savagery.

Then, I'm not sure what happened but Lena jumped up from the table and began to, rather abruptly, clear the dishes—I was expecting Ivan would have a staff, or maybe they were off for the evening—and I asked if I could help and Lena said no, it was taken care of, so maybe they were simply invisible. Lena could be abrasive, though there was something refreshing about a woman who said whatever it was she was thinking. And there was something familiar about her, a way of rejecting everything before it rejected her first.

LUKA AND I LEFT OUR WINDOWS OPEN TO THE AIR. IVAN did not believe in screens, as aesthetically unappealing as solar panels, but we opened the windows right into the night. Luka would have preferred them closed but he knew I could not sleep without fresh air. So the next morning we were both bitten, though Luka had only a few small bites, whereas my body looked completely ravaged. Mosquitoes, or some kind of tiny gnat that left welts on my body the size of grapes.

Luka was moody that morning, rare for him. He rubbed his eyes and this gesture made me recall a time I'd seen him cry. We'd both been in Athens, and I'd been waiting for him at a wine bar across from the Metropolitan Cathedral, where, at ten at night, a huge line had formed outside. I thought a famous person had died—this happens when a body lies in rest, say—but it was because the famous Axion Esti icon had been there, from Mount Athos. The chanting from the cathedral filled the square. He found me, fifteen minutes late, and he was crying.

I thought something terrible had happened. He was not Orthodox, or religious, but it didn't matter, I guess. It had reminded him of something. Now, the thought made a knot form in my throat and I found him shaving in the bathroom, a towel around his waist, and wrapped my arms around him.

Hi, he said.

I wore a short-sleeved dress to breakfast, but it still showed my legs, and I could feel some of the others eyeing me, as though there was something wrong with me.

That night, Ivan threw a bigger party, inviting more friends who lived nearby, and others who came in for the night. His large terrace filled with bodies and the mood felt joyous and the tension from the night before had defused. There were musicians playing a raucous, punky, hot-club-style jazz, which I loved—and found it hard not to dance to, though when some of the guests jumped up, Ivan shot them a look, which I supposed meant we were to appreciate but not enjoy ourselves too much?

Far in the distance I could see several terra-cotta-tiled roofs, and a view like this made me want to shout something out into the distance. But what? I was reminded again of that rooftop party where I'd encountered Luka.

I told Luka how much it reminded me of the view from my family house (my only house), from whose roof you could see mountains in one direction and the clear, glittering sea in the other. As I said it I had this feeling I'd left a stove on, the water running, the windows open in the rain. A child in the back seat, an animal I'd forgotten to feed, my keys on the kitchen table instead of in my coat pocket. An exam in a class I'd forgotten to attend. And who knows what was going on with my email.

There was a lot of wine, and a pitcher of cocktails. The day had been warm but the evening felt chilly. I had a drink and Luka had two and his usually dark eyes glittered, almost amber gold like whiskey, and it gave me a strange feeling again, as if I were seeing something I should not. Not a secret, but something from another time, like there was another layer on the evening. Any hint of tension had lifted and I wondered if I had imagined it; you could tell he and Ivan had a long history, that they ate bread and salt, as we'd say in Greek.

The musicians had finished playing and now were circulating. Ivan played music through the sound system, turning it up, as if now he was willing us all to dance, and Luka's moodiness had vanished. He was a great dancer—how had I not known that? He wrapped his arm around my waist and swung me around to the music, song after song. Everyone went nuts for Khaled's "C'est la vie" and I felt euphoric, dancing, singing, and we ended with Leonard Cohen's "Dance Me to the End of Love," which I hadn't heard for decades. I saw Ivan and Lena looking pointedly at us, but when I turned again they were talking with some of the other guests. I'd probably imagined it.

I was not drunk but I was cheerfully buzzed and I was aware of this moment as a moment that was happening now and would never happen again.

Luka tossed me into a spin and I lost my footing and crashed through Kathryn and Philip, nearly knocking Ivan over, but he caught me, as if it had been choreographed, and dipped me low to the floor.

I can see you are very happy here, Ivan said to me, and for the rest of the evening, I enjoyed myself.

At eleven o'clock sharp, the music stopped. Lights out, and Ivan and Lena said good night and disappeared. It was odd, to me; I did not know what to do next, they all seemed used to this abruptness. Kathryn and Philip left too, and Luka asked if I wanted a nightcap, but I had already had too much to drink, so the two of us sat on the small balcony of our room, the only room besides Ivan's that had a balcony, which he had made sure to note as he brought our things in there. Luka brought up two mugs of tea and a little glass of whiskey, and we sat together, looking quietly at the night.

When we got into bed, Luka looked at me with seriousness.

The Americans keep placing the bread on their plates, he said.

I looked into his eyes, so deep and brown and playful.

Ivan mentioned this to me, he added.

Should I ask them to leave? I finally said.

And then he laughed: a big, loud laugh.

THE NEXT MORNING THE SIGHT OF LUKA'S TAN FEET stretching out from the sheets gave me the sense I might never see him again, and I was overcome with feeling. The bed that had at first seemed comfortable and grand now was hurting my back.

I rose to open the balcony shutters and got back into bed. From that room you could see the olive groves and the lavender fields. The world still hazy, both fully formed and still emerging; the figures on the sea could be boats or dolphins or trees.

Luka took a drink of water and handed me a glass. My hairbrush was on the nightstand and I ran it through my hair, a gesture that gave me that uncanny sense again, but I did feel better.

I could see the whiskey had affected him, though; he was really only a beer and wine drinker, and last night's cheer and levity lifted from the top of his back and hovered there. He was reading something on his phone, only one eye open, the way he read disturbing news in the morning, to make it easier to look away. I settled my head in his lap. I opened my eyes and looked up at him and for a moment I saw another man's face entirely.

Did it upset you, I asked him, when those guests—? I trailed off.

No, he said. He got up and disappeared into the bathroom.

When Luka emerged from the shower, he stood next to the bed, hand on his hip, like a soccer player. It wasn't that it upset me, the question, he said. My work reminds me of war every day. Catastrophes are not only in the past, for one, and only small countries are reduced to them. We're headed toward them too.

He sat on the bed, smoothing my hair out of my face. His voice was not angry but gentle. It's not like I ever forget and I'm suddenly reminded. It's not triggering. He gave an ironic smirk around the word, for my American benefit.

You'd think people who were so scared to say anything untoward would think to not ask such a thing at a dinner party, in this country. What is it with such obsession with other people's pain—as if they too want to seize it, as if pain is all there is here. As if they have been somehow cheated to not have had strife, he added.

I'm sorry, I said.

It's not you.

It is though, I said.

Before that, they were talking about a nearby island that's gone plastic free.

Oh? I said.

Why is it so baffling that we'd protect our riches? Besides, he said. What does it matter. Human violence and our obsession with power will ruin us first.

I could see something in him, something of his spirit, which seemed to open up to enclose me within it, the way the tide might suddenly sweep away your beach bag, your book; you look up and see your sandal bobbing about in the tide. Something chaotic. But by the time we joined the others for breakfast, Luka's mood had shifted, the cloud that had hung over him seemed to have lifted, that chasm had sealed itself.

But I thought about his words a lot.

In the afternoon I dressed in a new bathing suit—navy blue—and went to the pool, which looked over the valley to one end and the sea in the distance on the other, and wondered about the inclusion of pools in places like this, with such access to the sea. I knew they'd been common in ancient

Greece but when introduced to the modern country they were unpopular: All that stagnant water had associations with the tombs, with death.

Years ago, one November visiting Athens, I'd made the mistake of diving into an outdoor unheated hotel pool. The water was ice and I felt my heart seize up, and thought for a moment my heart had stopped. Two members of the housekeeping staff stopped to watch me, as in, You have got to see this. But another Greek woman sitting at the small café tables, having a cigarette with her coffee, advised me to do this each morning and I'd be young forever. Even better if in the sea. Another woman sat nearby, reading the paper, but didn't seem to notice anything at all.

In Ivan's pool I swam a lazy freestyle, back and forth, back and forth. The pool was long enough for swimming laps but short enough that you could never find a good rhythm. After several laps, I felt that someone was watching me, and I stopped at the wall to adjust my goggles.

Lena now stood on the pool deck. I could tell she was waiting for me to acknowledge her, so I stopped and looked up, greeting her, squinting into the sun. She was in a boxy burgundy dress that made her look elegant and cozy and thin and I felt cold and naked and happily fed.

I wasn't sure if I should apologize. Was I not supposed to be in the pool? Maybe there were opening hours. I wouldn't put it past Ivan.

Can I give you a tip? she said.

I was used to unsolicited advice on how to be from certain aristocratic-acting women who always treated me as though I'd just left the village on a donkey.

You're not kicking, she said. You should get some fins.

Thank you, I said. I'll try. I didn't tell her I often swam with fins.

It'll really tone your thighs, she added. She gestured to her assortment of swim gear, which sat on a little shelf behind a small bar. Help yourself. I thanked her but didn't take her up on it.

My thighs, honestly, were just fine. I'd been swimming my entire life; I knew about kicking. I was not flip turning—the short distance of the pool made me dizzy—but when I completed another lap I did not stop to allow her to say Much better but instead turned in an aggressive flip. I swam another twenty minutes, kicking very hard. When I finished my swim, she was gone.

What was wrong with me.

AFTER, I SHOWERED AND DRESSED AND WANDERED DOWNstairs, peered into the library that was full of books but seemed unused. I didn't mean to barge in on Ivan and Luka, where they were standing on either side of a desk, and Ivan had some papers in front of him. They both looked up at me when I entered. I apologized but they didn't seem bothered, they both smiled at me and we walked out together.

Later, a group was making an excursion with Ivan's boat to the caves. Luka asked if I wanted to go, but the thought alone made me claustrophobic. I told him I was not interested in small spaces, in entrances to the underworld—I did not mean this to be funny but he laughed. I loved to swim but I preferred to stay atop the water, my body inhabited by that blending of sea and sky. Besides the huge ferries I relied on to move about, I did not care for boats, or I liked boats but not the people they traveled with, those people who docked in the harbor.

I told him he could go but he said, honestly, he didn't want to, and we had a relaxing day by the pool, had lunch on our own in the small seaside town, and left in midafternoon.

On the drive back, Luka was chatty. Something I do a couple of times a year, he said, Ivan's parties. He didn't add anything else so I didn't pry, but I detected a sense of obligation, duty, a friendship with a power imbalance. I sensed I'd walked in on something between the two men: a request, an obligation, something outside my frame of reference.

I know one of Lena's translators, he said.

Yeah? How was their experience? I asked.

Oh, he said. Can you imagine? He looked over at me with that conspiratorial look.

Thanks for bringing me along, I said, looking straight ahead, because when I looked at him while he was driving he had the impulse to face me, which was often a little disconcerting on these roads.

Yeah?

Yeah, I said.

He reached over and ran his hand over my cheek, and I recalled the Beckett play and the bodies in dirt, waiting to be unearthed. I thought of all those things we bury and excavate, including ourselves.

WHEN WE RETURNED I FINALLY FINISHED THE TRANSLA-tion, working at great speed, feeling as though the book were unraveling and I was chasing it down a long staircase while trying to pull a dress over my head. The woman tells her friend that she thinks he's jealous of the biologist's falcon the way he might be jealous of a rival lover. That he speaks of the creature with a bit of disdain, dismissal. She tells him he's acting obsessively, and the man then refuses to talk to his friend, the woman who is narrating, so she loses the story. He disappears.

One weekend, the narrator goes to her island, the island where the biologist happens to work. Not only is the man there, as she suspected; she finds him living in her house, so obsessed with being near the biologist, and so ashamed of his obsession, that he didn't even bother to ask if he might stay in her house. She would have said yes. He'd stayed there with her before and knew where she hid a spare key, and she was surprised at his ability to walk right in as though it were his. He probably charmed the neighbors, which made them suspect nothing. Somehow, he felt entitled to it, to mill about the house even though his friend was not there. Or maybe because she was not there.

But she doesn't kick him out and instead goes about her own business: inviting friends over, going out, checking in on her parents, who live nearby. As if dealing with a band of suitors, she accepts him there and continues her daily life around him, and, reluctantly, he resumes telling her his story, as if it's now her burden to receive it.

And then the beloved falcon disappears, its tracking device gone and all traces of its physical presence, at around the same time a mysterious yacht appears in the distance. This yacht looms off the coast like an apparition, a yacht larger than the villages of the island, a yacht whose vastness the narrator cannot get her mind around. Rumors flow like lava; everyone wonders about its owner. A head of state in exile, it's a war criminal, it's a team of foreign operatives, it's a crown prince, it's a secret energy company wanting to drill for oil. It's an Onassis, it's a Latsis, it's a whole town of refugees. It's some other shipping tycoon. A big-time musician, trying to find inspiration in some local music? The pop star who became a billionaire by the age of twenty-five? The famous actor couple, no, they'd never be so gauche, besides, they have a house on a nearby island. The speculations go on and on.

The narrator, though, suspects her friend. That somehow he wanted to hurt the biologist, sabotage her career.

In my mind, as I was translating, this character became the ferryman. I could see in the text his intense face, except his face was gone now, the way we both deeply see the face of a character when we read and also see just wisps and fragments: a curtain of hair, a long nose, the sweep of a dress.

At first, the yacht is an object of curiosity, something the villagers talk about in the plateia or the hair salon or among the women who run the little boutiques in the alleyways, who seem to know everything. It's all anyone talks about, on the white beaches and the blue taverna chairs in the sand, up in the castro, in those villages up at the top of the island, where from certain points you can see the ship too. The grocery store, which is the epicenter of all stories. At the distillery and at the old tavernas up in the mountain villages that cook a pig on a spit.

The narrator calls it the *Oligarch* and grows more obsessed with it, allowing it to eclipse the interest she has in her friend and his love life, a friend who has taken up residence in her house. She searches online, calls the marine authority, wonders if she can figure out its provenance. From the narrator's balcony, which she is now sharing with her friend, she stares at it as if it were part of the landscape, another rock, a lighthouse, a caldera, the moon.

The island gossip goes on and on, and the more they all talk about the yacht the more mysterious it becomes. Then one day it's gone, and no one saw it leave; as if it did not set sail in the night but disappeared into air. Things unravel.

The novel ends with the biologist breaking it off with the man; he goes back to Athens, and she and her daughter sit on the narrator's terrace, looking out at the sea, the gaping hole the yacht has left when it departed.

I felt gutted when I finished, hollowed out, when those last words of the novel moved through my fingertips onto the page. Later, I would tell Luka about it, but it was Marta, I thought, who would appreciate the story most. I'd wait to send it to her, when it was a real book, bound between covers, a real, new thing.

THE NIGHT I FINISHED THE FIRST DRAFT OF THE TRANSLAtion, Luka and I sat on a bench watching the sun plunge into the sea. I felt bereft, at a loss for what to do next. I did not feel like going back to the beginning. When we tell a story, we know the ending, that's why we tell it, but that hadn't been the case here, so no matter the ending, it would have caught me off guard. I had learned the ending as I was translating it on the page.

Luka said anytime he finished anything he felt both emptiness and relief, and that emerging from the days and hours spent on a clip that ran for five minutes was the most difficult. Here and then gone. He told me he was nearly done with his novel, too, about to turn in the final draft, and felt himself stalling, avoiding its completion. I remembered what Marta had said, about his novel being sad.

A melancholy ending? I asked.

Not sure, he said, and looked at me as though the answer was contained in my face.

Four sailboats docked under the supermoon, and nearby a larger boat anchored.

Would you call that a yacht? I asked, and my voice felt uncanny, like it had come out of Luka's body. For a moment I saw a past and future unfolding against the pink and purple light of the late evening, the patches of glassy turquoise water next to those midnight-blue depths.

A catamaran, Luka said. We watched for a while as someone on a small dinghy moved between the sailboats, running people to the shore, and then between boats. It was amusing to watch; there was a joy to it. The setting sun cast the boats and the people into silhouettes, giving them an eerie shadow-puppet quality. I had the memory of being at another port in another place with him, looking out at the sailboats, but I could not place the where or the when. That memory, that self, lived in that space between object and shadow, emerging only at certain moments, depending on the relationship to body and light. Was that the version of me in his novel? I didn't know what was what anymore: translation, novel, body, self.

We were silent awhile.

I'm getting a new car, he said, finally.

That's great, I said.

I've had this one for decades. Fine for around town, he added, as if embarrassed by this act of consumption.

What will you do with the old one?

He shrugged. It's too old to sell, he said.

I could buy it from you, I said.

I would never take money from you. I would give it to you.

Only Luka would just offer to give me his car. The most generous people are always the ones who have lost a lot.

Then he seemed to reconsider. What if it broke down and stranded you somewhere? he asked. I'd feel terrible.

I do want to buy a car when I return to Greece, I said. Something small and inexpensive, several years old. To keep at the house.

Luka paused. It was the first time I'd acknowledged to him that I'd at some point return to Greece.

What kind of car are you thinking? I asked, and he readily named a few, as if he'd been waiting for someone to ask him that question.

WHEN LUKA DROPPED ME OFF, NEDA WAITED FOR ME ON the landing. Arms crossed, seated in a wooden chair placed there for that purpose. Granddaughter, she said. I would love something sweet.

Of course, I said. The bakery was closed but I told her I had something upstairs, that I'd be right back. She nodded, pleased. How long had she been waiting there for me, for anyone?

I was touched by her use of the word "granddaughter," even if she was confused. I was closer to the age of her daughter. My grandparents had all been gone a long time, both sets, but sometimes missing them felt so palpable and new. I recalled a moment watching the news with my Ukrainian grandmother, footage of lines of Bosnian refugees, and even though her English was not strong, she could barely stay in the room. There was no language for such atrocity anyway, and she studied the screen, the faces, as if she might, impossible, see a cousin or the parents and brother she left behind.

It was the first time I sensed that chronological distance did not always bring solace, and that history was not only temporal but spatial. Years could be housed within other years, weeks housed within weeks, suddenly reappearing through the unearthing of bones.

When the camera focused on a young, worried face of a pregnant woman and her husband, my grandmother smacked her hand to her chest. Like we were, she said. At the time I saw it as compassion and then as a pernicious memory that rose up, unwanted, and now I saw it as something subterranean, an eerie recognition that blurred the boundaries of time or space.

But it was this gesture, hitting her breast, that she did when scared or relieved, something she said she did when pregnant with my mother, having narrowly escaped some bombs.

Together with a group, running one way, and she, always with a sense of things, made them all stop course and go the other way. Within minutes their previous destination had gone up in smoke. That was the story she told, about hitting her chest. My mother was born with a raised birthmark there, above her breast, that my grandmother swore was from that moment. My mother had it removed. I don't have a birthmark, but I do have a small constellation of dark, tiny freckles on my chest that my grandmother used to say was part of that same slap. But when startled I whack myself like that; I have as long as I remember. At some point, I must have told this all to Luka.

I returned to Neda's place with something I'd purchased earlier, on a whim: small, delicate-looking layer cakes. Neda was no longer on the landing but her door was still open. I peered in her apartment and she was preparing tea for us both.

She praised my choice, called me a good girl, and placed two little cakes onto two light green plates. It was delicious.

When I first met Lyuba, it had been here, at the apartment, and I'd assumed she lived there with her mother. She lived nearby and visited often, even stayed from time to time. She wanted her mother to move in with her and her husband, but Neda, it seemed, refused to move. I was happy to check in on her. It is much easier to take care of someone you are not obligated to take care of.

Now, Neda seemed tired. I asked if she wanted to rest, and she said yes.

I haven't done the morning chores, she said. The animals.

I'm sorry?

She brought the plates to the sink, and I washed them for her. I remembered it was better to go along with these harmless questions, so as not to confuse her, or worse, frighten her. Oh, yes. They're safe.

I used to swim each morning, like you, she said.

I smiled and waited for her to tell me more.

How long are you staying? she asked.

Once more, I didn't know how to answer. Did she mean in this country or in her apartment? I could answer the latter but not the former.

Go now, so I can rest.

ONE NIGHT, LUKA AND I WERE HAVING DINNER AT MY place; I made stuffed peppers and I'd bought a few more of those layer cakes. Madjarica, they were called.

I woke in the middle of the night to the sound of a train and Neda knocking on my door. It's the poyizd, she said. The Ukrainian word for train. You'll be late. Her cries became more plaintive and frantic. The train was louder and maybe it was not a train but the horn of the ferry, though what ferries were leaving in the middle of the night? I finally got out of bed and opened the door for her but she was not there, there was no one there. Everything was quiet.

I returned to bed, mumbling to Luka about the sound of the train and the poyizd, the way I never used the English word, how a train at night could never be anything but the word my grandmother used, and the train had woken me up. And then I recalled something else my grandmother would say when I was exhibiting disorderly conduct: Remember yourself! she'd say, as if I had somehow dismembered myself, disassembled myself, as if my bad behavior had simply been an act of both deconstructing and forgetting, and come to think of it, isn't that exactly the truth? She was not asking for a remembering but a recognition: of what I was doing, whom I was affecting, and to see myself in two places at once, the person I was inhabiting and the one who'd become a stranger to me.

There are no trains here, Luka was saying, it's an island.

Did you not hear Neda? I asked.

Luka smoothed my hair out of my face and took my hand. Neda would have said "vlak," he said gently.

Oh, I said. Greeks, especially in the north, used that word too.

Go back to sleep, he said, you were dreaming.

Maybe it was the ferry? I asked. I went to the window, even though I knew I could not see the sea.

It's three a.m. He put his hand on my head.

He was wrong, I thought. I was still so sure of it.

But I slept long and hard after that, and when I opened the shutters and the day was bright and stretching toward noon, Luka was gone.

Eleni Vakalo writes and Karen Emmerich translates: "Do you really know whether you're inside or out / Of the closed spaces that always exist?"

Luka had made no mention of having to leave early that morning. He had a few trips planned for work and research, but I couldn't remember which was next. Luka had always intuited my discomfort with steadiness and permanence and having to make plans too far in advance. And I also understood this about him.

I made the bed, turned on the stove, made an espresso in the small red pot. I folded and put away some brightly colored dish towels and felt a pang of nostalgia, already missing something before it was gone.

It was not strange for us not to talk during the day, when we were both working, and when he was working on something, he tended to lose track of time. That's what I told myself, anyway.

I texted him the next day, but nothing. In our years before it was not unusual for us to have email or text conversations that were drawn out over several weeks, as though we were sending letters, but that was before. This summer there had been very few messages between us; usually he just showed up, or I went there, and there was not a lot of back-and-forth. This summer had no paper trail.

I tried again the next day, and the next, but these messages did not seem to go through, and I began to understand this new reality, an end that had come as seamlessly as our relationship began. Texting Marta to see if she had heard from him felt invasive, or maybe embarrassing; I didn't have Ivan's number but probably wouldn't text him anyway.

I WALKED THE HALF KILOMETER TO LUKA'S APARTMENT and sat in the nearby café, where we often sat. I loved its green chairs. Those mornings it was nearly impossible to get a table but also exciting to have done so. During the week the vibe was cool and unhurried and it made sense that this was Luka's favorite place.

It was a popular café, not particularly touristy; you were more likely to see the families who lived in that town, who owned restaurants and hotels or had been coming here for generations. The sort of place people chose for their Saturday outings, dressed to be seen. Everyone seemed to know everyone, and no one was speaking English. Across the square was a large church. I watched all the local children emerge from their First Communion service, the girls dressed head to toe in white, like nuns, and the boys in tan robes and sandals like Saint Francis of Assisi.

I looked up at Luka's balcony, half expecting to see him come out and stretch. I ordered a double espresso, even though lately I'd been drinking café au lait. It sounded good, and familiar, and I had never really liked milk, had I? The street was quiet, and I finished my coffee and drank my water, jotting notes down in my journal. I was steeling myself to walk into his building, into his flat. He'd given me his keys, after all, to both the flat and his car, yet to use them unannounced seemed like an act of trespassing. He hadn't asked me, this time, to water his plants.

I was on my second coffee when the door to Luka's building opened and a couple emerged: young, nicely dressed, holding hands. They chatted with a woman dressed in a camel-colored suit, wide-leg trousers, very sharp. Both women wore their honey-colored hair long and straight, and the man's hair was black and wavy. The apartment was above a flower shop, but the staircase that led to it was private; it had been his alone.

As they moved closer to the café, I could hear their conversation: The woman in the suit seemed to be a real estate agent. I watched the young couple talk excitedly with the woman, their eyes darting around the narrow street, peering around the corner, wondering if this could be a home. I wondered what brought people here, and how long they'd planned to stay. They were speaking English but with an accent, maybe German or Dutch, so for them maybe everything here was a bargain. They said they'd be in touch and they hurried off.

The woman checked a few messages on her phone.

I'm sorry, I said, I don't speak very well—please excuse my mistakes.

She waved her hand the way people always did, said, Do not worry, you speak very well.

Are you showing the apartment? I saw it was available.

I pretended I could not speak as well as I could, so she might think I didn't have the words for "on the internet" or "advertised in the newspaper" or "call for a showing" or whatever. She looked around, as though she had really been looking forward to her coffee and quiet and was trying to assess my seriousness. Though as I spoke I felt my already-tenuous language skills slipping, and I didn't have to pretend.

It doesn't have to be now, of course. Perhaps we can make an appointment?

No, no, she said. Now is very good. I will be happy to show you. Let me send a message to the owner and I'll be right with you.

Okay, I said. Thank you.

He likes to know about a showing before it happens.

I had assumed Luka owned the apartment, an investment, a summer place, but honestly I was not sure. Maybe he'd come here when first divorced. I paid for my coffees and the two of us went back to the apartment. For all I knew it was Ivan's.

I followed her up the stairs, listening to her talk about the place, the light.

Inside the small apartment, the furniture was all there, though stripped of anything intimate. I had thought of his place as spare and minimalist, but it had simply been organized and efficient. Now it felt empty. The large desk was still beneath the window, but the fluffy white rug was gone, and the place smelled faintly of industrial-strength cleaners.

The boxes of herbs and the large ferns were still on the balcony, but the three plants—his favorites—that sat atop the small table were gone. Instead of Luka's gray duvet, the bed was covered with a white bedspread. I opened a kitchen cupboard and it was empty. The counters of course were clean and clear: no papers, no coffee cups, none of the little notebooks where Luka used to write down this and that, sudden ideas he'd have in the middle of a conversation. No tall stacks of books.

When the real estate agent took a call on the balcony, I walked back inside into the bathroom, which was clean, with two white hand towels and a small, newly unwrapped olive oil soap. The dresser drawers were cleared but in the bottom drawer, crammed in the back, nearly falling behind the drawer, was Luka's soft gray sweatshirt. I pulled it out and tied it around my shoulders. I remembered him in it though couldn't recall when.

I peered out onto the balcony, where the real estate agent was still talking on the phone, her back to me. The awning had been rolled back, which it never had been. I had not noticed from the perspective of the café, but out here the balcony felt exposed and vulnerable in the brightness. I looked down at the street, at the small table where I'd been sitting.

I caught a glimpse of my shadow and it startled me, as though it might pull me into some other world, the world I was supposed to be in and maybe also was. I cast another glance across the large open room, the kitchen, the bedroom, to see if I might find traces of him, of us. But I'd known, somehow, that I'd been cleaved from a reality that was playing itself out somewhere else. All this had been temporary. I had left nothing behind.

I'm not sure about it, I told the woman. I've just started looking. But thank you for showing me.

She asked for my name and I gave it to her, though now I cannot remember which name I used. I combined into something new. If I'd given the one Luka called me, the character of his novel, he would know I had come here, poking around. If he indeed was the owner. But why wouldn't I come looking for him? And if I had given my own name, would it be one he recognized? I didn't know what was what anymore.

We walked down the stairs together. Sometimes when I'd leave, Luka would walk me down, lingering there by the door, or follow me out to pick up some groceries, the newspapers, and when I got to the bottom of the stairs, I turned, as if to see him once more. But of course it was just the real estate agent, looking at me strangely. I felt translucent again. If she noticed the sweatshirt, though, she didn't mention it.

That weekend at Ivan's, I'd walked in on the two of them in the library, their heads bent close together, talking about something. Somehow I thought it had to do with his departure, his apartment, but I'm not sure why. Just a feeling.

I walked from Luka's to the old town. The narrow alleyways were busy; a ferry had just arrived. Locals out for their morning errands, their groceries, their banking. Already on that bright early morning, so many bodies crowded the harbor that I thought it would submerge. If one more person, one more tiny dog, one more set of luggage came off a boat or appeared from down a narrow passageway, poof! We would sink into a subterranean world, read the strata of sand and history, swim through a thick underwater lake, move through a silent echoless cave, and flow through the stream of ocean like stories, like language, the secret rivers that race under this sea: one saltwater moving inland, and a freshwater river escaping below it, unable to be tapped.

THE NEXT MORNING, QUITE EARLY, LUKA MESSAGED, BUT on another platform. I was walking to the cove for my swim.

Hi! he said. This was how he'd always responded to me, when I messaged him out of the blue, when we hadn't been in touch for months, years. As if the reminder of my existence was a delight.

And sometimes I would simply respond the same: Hi! And there would be no other conversation for another week or month.

Where are you? I wrote now. I wanted to ask, Are you alive?

[. . .] [. . .] [. . .] My stomach tightened.

Did you swim? he wrote.

On my way.

[. . .] [. . .]

I read the exchange again and again, waiting for more typing. He hadn't said where he was, though I understood maybe he did not want to note. I wanted to ask for how long, I wanted to ask where. Maybe he knew I'd gone to his apartment.

New assignment, I said.

Yes, he wrote.

I asked him how it was going and he said it was okay, and I told him, Be safe, and he responded: Kisses.

That was that.

I felt relief and realized now I'd been afraid he was dead.

BUT AFTER THAT, NO MORE WORD FROM LUKA, NO. WHAT was always good between us was our ability to read subtext. Direct communication is best, they say, but I think it's overrated. Sometimes there's something less literal, something invisible you both can see. Everything exists in the subtext anyway; if I did not know this as a writer, I knew it as a translator. With translation, though, it couldn't be just a hunch. You had to understand all the possible meanings. With Luka I never understood all the possible meanings and interpretations, but it was like the conversations I had when I was first learning the language, a layer of familiarity already living somewhere in my brain. Yet I felt my comprehension slipping.

What did it feel like when you knew a relationship was over? Well, maybe this was one of the ways. Comprehension slipping.

Around three in the morning, I awoke to the sound again, this time definitely the call of a ferry. Only then did I recall that it had also happened the night before. I'd slept through it, allowing the sound to become the border of my dreams, but this time it fully woke me.

The next morning, I walked to the harbor; the catamaran was gone. The four sailboats in the distance gone too. One small fishing boat, the one that was usually there, puttered toward the beach, where the tide was on its way out. The boat's owner was a smiling, handsome guy with a close-trimmed beard and a nice body, people were always turning to admire him, about my age. He always said hi to me when he saw me out and about.

Today he looked at me with a bit of sadness, as though he knew something about my life that I did not. I tried to piece things together, searched for moments I'd missed, replayed conversations looking for clues. It was no use. The demand to know, to ask questions, to have things explained; it seemed Luka and I had lived outside these boundaries. As if we could ever truly know someone, ever truly know ourselves, as if there was even a difference.

I went by Luka's apartment and saw his old car still parked where it was usually parked, in the open lot near the dumpsters, not far from the taxi stands. His own street was too narrow and he hated having to look for parking. He preferred to always leave it in the same place. And always unlocked, which drove me nuts but he didn't understand the big deal. I got in and opened the glove box and flipped through the leather case, where I knew he kept a set of car keys. I took them, just in case. In the back seat I had a pair of sunglasses, a few books, and a beach bag. And there were his three beloved plants. He'd told me what they were called, but now I could not remember. I pulled them out to take them with me, leaving the rest of my things in the back seat. Then I locked his car and walked back home.

NEDA WAS WAITING FOR ME AGAIN ON THE WOODEN CHAIR in the stairwell and I wished I'd thought to stop at the bakery. She stood when I appeared and handed me a little plastic bag, printed with an embroidery pattern. Inside was an old-style swim cap, cream-colored and printed with large, raised flowers, a chin strap. I felt a wave swell up and crest inside me. I gave her one of the plants, remembering how she'd found such joy in watering the ones outside. She set it down and gave me a hug, taking care not to crush the other two plants between us.

Then she asked: What happened to the man? There were times her words seemed a bit slurred, and though my comprehension had gotten good by then, I still of course made errors in speech, imagined false cognates, understood a word to mean one thing when it meant nothing of the sort. I was always mishearing things. Some days I sailed through conversation and other days I struggled to utter a complete sentence. So when she spoke again, I thought she said something about missing me, but it could also have been something about a forest.

I asked her to repeat, but she was quiet and pulled her hug away, looking me straight in the eyes and speaking a phrase I am absolutely certain I did not misunderstand:

Remember yourself, she said.

For a while I'd been somehow freed from worry about disappointment or anger, though it threatened to break through my subconscious to the surface from time to time. So how disconcerting to feel it all back again, as if it had hovered around me all along, waiting for me to recognize it so it could bear down on my chest.

THAT NIGHT, I AWOKE IN A TERROR, UNABLE TO MOVE. MY body felt heavy and my mind so foggy that I struggled to remember my name. A blank feeling that I've felt only a few times in my life but the memory of which is still chilling. I reached over to the other side of the bed, searching for someone, but could not think of who. I tried to speak, no sound. I tried to piece together my previous day: a vague sense of memory of a visit with Neda. Had I gone swimming? Had I spoken to anyone else?

In my forties I had gotten migraines that affected my vision: white bands over the image, as if they were censoring something from my line of sight. Now it was as if swaths of my day had disappeared. Finally I was able to move to turn on the light on my nightstand, and watched my hands open and close a fist, open and close. Luka came to mind, but I'm not convinced that he was who I was looking for. Something, someone, deeper in the past.

The flat, despite all my things strewn about, began to feel not only temporary but detached from my reality, as if when inside it I didn't exist at all. I had that strange thought again: I'm in a box.

I rose from bed and drank a glass of water and then another. I went out to the balcony, propped my elbows on the railing, looked down onto the narrow residential street. Earlier that evening two Fiats had been at an impasse—you weren't supposed to drive down this street at all. Now, the street was quiet. I felt suspended in a limbo that was compressing me into itself; I had the sense that I was disappearing, that if I stayed put I would be gone in the morning. It was bizarre and illogical, I knew. But I had to go, now or never.

I quickly took down the laundry I'd left drying overnight and folded it atop the bed. And then I began to place it not into my drawers but into my suitcase, nearly frantically, as though I were about to miss a plane. But I had no plane ticket, no plans. I had to take the wheel and drive.

Across the narrow street was the little bakery that filled my room with the smell of bread each morning. Now, close to three in the morning, it was dark, though I knew within the hour there'd be a light on inside. The owners lived above it and sometimes, late afternoons, maybe after their naps, they sat on their balcony with cold tumblers of water between them, or rakija, or a pot of tea.

There was music in the distance. I heard footsteps, the trot of clogs on the cobblestone. The light above the bakery's sign illuminated the entire street, and with the light of the moon, I could see a woman approaching. Familiar, like the woman from the theater, the woman who'd left at the same time. Or maybe she was the woman who swam with me, the one afraid of the jellyfish. She wore jeans and a blue button-up shirt. Flat brown sandals, the kind they sold in the markets. The look on her face was ruminative, dreamy, and she walked quickly but not necessarily with purpose or direction.

She didn't seem like a tourist but a local, walking home, in no hurry. Her hair fell in large, floppy curls past her shoulders, as I once wore mine, and she carried an over-the-shoulder bag that looked way too heavy; it seemed to be pulling her to one side. She held a bunch of lavender, a little perplexing at that hour, but she could have gathered it herself, or been given a gift. Perhaps she'd been out all day, was coming back from drinks by the sea, moving with her own grace, her flowers, long after midnight.

Perhaps like me. Perhaps me.

I wanted to get her attention, I wanted her to see me up there, but didn't know why, or what to say, so I called out my name. At first nothing came out, my voice was blocked. Again I tried and it emerged, inflected with the pronunciation and version not of my language but of this one, a small translation, an accent, a shift of vowels and consonants. My voice did not sound like my own but it emerged, not too loudly but she must have heard because she stopped and looked up, shielding her eyes as if the sun were shining. I waited to see if she recognized me, if she recognized herself in that name.

Oh, I said, I'm sorry, I thought you were someone else.

I is someone else, she said, or maybe I said it? We both laughed, though I could tell I flustered her.

Where are you going? I asked.

Home, she said. Where else? She walked away, and I felt bad for having disturbed her peace.

Still, I wondered what I had looked like to her from that angle: a shadow, a figure, a woman who'd climbed up the text of a page and teetered at the top. A woman suspended on a balcony in the middle of the night.

I HAD TO LEAVE. THE URGE FELT FIERCE. TO WHERE, though? Back to Greece; the house was empty now. I would go there. I finished packing and I scrubbed the apartment spotless and before sunrise I dragged my luggage, and the two plants, through the pedestrian streets, down to the bus station and the lot where Luka kept his car. It had seemed that I'd accumulated so many things, but once I packed it all away it didn't seem like much at all. The taxi stands and the port were packed: the promenade along the water, the rows of yachts and people taking photos of the yachts, even the square near the cathedral, where all the locals sat.

Hadn't I told myself after this trip I'd stop flying so much? What I wanted was to travel by sea, to keep my eye on both land and water at once. It would have been geographically logical that a ferry would connect us, these two countries that welcomed so many tourists, but geopolitically difficult. Besides, such an easy route might put the already too-high tourist numbers over the edge. Still, in my imagination I could leave from that northern Adriatic port and sail down to the Ionian. But there were no easy connections. I'd have to drive, or sail first to Italy. I lacked a pilot. If only I could commandeer a boat and its crew, or build my own raft and sail the gentle waves home.

Of course, this is not a story about logic. It's a story about theme and variation and echo, told not to re-create what happened or even what could have happened but to create a happening on the page. About what it all felt like. Not the creation of story but its decreation. A self you unravel to its ante-self, and then put back together again and hope the filigree patches of gold make it glow. With the understanding that this seam is the only self and it is like the seashore, never fixed and never the same.

But even then I did understand one thing: All that was to help me remember myself, to recognize myself. But to remember myself made me feel like someone else, a stranger, and maybe that was the point. Re-member and re-know. Not about asserting a self but a sort of unselfing. To become a new original. To move through a space and become something again. To put my hands on the wheel and drive.

MAYBE LUKA'D WANTED THE CAR TO DISAPPEAR, AS HE HAD disappeared. Maybe I'd wanted a marker of something, a physical artifact of that time, a reminder—car, sweatshirt, keys, plants.

When I got inside his car, I felt my insides clench, the familiar knot in my throat. Luka's car was old but it smelled nice, like his soap.

Hadn't he, sort of, offered the car to me?

I don't know what possessed me. I knew this trip was very long. It mapped as fifteen hours but I knew that it would be much longer. In the States, I would fly this distance. And here I had several border crossings, and I had no idea what the roads were like. But I supposed I just needed to see the road in front of me. Like driving at night. So I loaded my things and drove away.

I drove the car out of that town and to the other port, the quiet one, through the long tunnel Luka and I had driven through, through where he'd become disoriented and asked me to drive those last several minutes to the ferry.

Again the tunnel went on and on.

My memory of it was the last memory, the way the tunnel had unnerved Luka. The road carved into the landscape with the sea down the gentle slopes, and at one point the road curved sharply, and was not prepared for it. A car coming from the other direction also swerved to avoid me, as if its driver had also forgotten the road.

I drove onto the first morning ferry at daybreak, like I had so many times but in another country and another life that waited for me at the bottom of this sea. Maybe this was how it was supposed to end between us, kaleidoscoping into the beginning.

Mary Ruefle writes: "You haven't even begun. You must pause first, the way one must always pause before a great endeavor, if only to take a good breath."

While driving, I tried to remember some lines of a song I'd heard at the festival: about missing the snowy mountains, about what I had always thought of in Greece as xenitia, otherness in a foreign land. There was a through line that also reminded me of a Greek song I'd danced to many nights, the ways these songs combined joy and sadness. In my mind now, I'd heard it that snowy night in the bar, after the carjacking, but I am not certain this is true. I could feel all my languages and cultures mixing about inside me, and somehow this song seemed to hold it all in. The songs were often about the songs, as they were in Greek rebetika: I am singing about the pain I sing about. The Greek verb "to feel pain" is not in the passive voice but active: "I hurt," or even, "I care for."

I glanced to my back seat, to Luka's plants.

While driving, Luka and I had sung along to the radio.

Traversing. Travel and verse.

I write the story of the unfinished story, I have taken the keys.

I emerged from the translation of *Occupation* into writing something else, something new. Yet I thought of it often, as though I had known the characters, had lived that life, had found a man I cared about living in my home as he tracked a woman who was tracking a falcon who had, most likely, been captured by the owner of a yacht. I'd been a long-term guest in the book.

I wanted to head for that coastal forest, to the thermal springs, to those umbrella pine trees that stretched to the sea. I wanted to see the waterfall, alive and alone. They say that water is healing and I don't think that's untrue, but what I have always been drawn to are the subversive qualities of the aquatic. That fine border between land and sea.

There's an energy there. Things transform.

I DROVE AND RESTED, I CROSSED BORDERS, I STOPPED TO take in the view. In Albania I thought I'd fly right off a cliff. The language, even though I'd heard it many times in Greece, felt unrecognizable to me. I played the CD I'd bought at the festival.

Folk has no national lines but it's appropriated to define national lines. The subjugation of the feminine for a masculine project. I remembered Luka, who had little interest in folk music, reacting with such surprise that I'd been so touched by it. It's a bit kitsch, he said. Then he told me that interrogators had played their national music to torture prisoners of other ethnicities. This I hadn't known. But the music stretched back way further, I said, before all that, no?

Well yeah, he said. I never paid much attention to it.

But you know all the songs, I said.

Well, true. He laughed.

But like Luka, I was suspicious of nation, I did not care about its borders and their assertion of uniqueness and purity, the flattening of all that lived inside them. Particularly of course when the assertion of uniqueness turned violent. It's why I loved those tremulous zones near borders, where everything seemed to blur, Greek language in Cyrillic, Slavic in Greek, Turkish in the Greek alphabet. The Bosnian Ladino folk songs we'd listened to at the festival, the list of songs that reminded me of Greek songs and probably all had been Ottoman. I'd recently read an interview with the famous author who'd been attacked onstage, in which he'd said that what he saw when he was stabbed were palaces made of alphabets. Palaces made of alphabets! I could not rid my mind of that image.

The roads were not always easy but better than I had imagined. I passed through the mulberry trees. Along one stretch, the olive groves tumble down to the shore; pollen scatters to the bottom of the sea.

I crossed rivers and rivulets. I expected checkpoints, or maybe even bored men targeting lone female foreigners. Sometimes the car made disconcerting noises and I remembered Luka saying he worried it wasn't safe. Because of my own impatience I almost ran out of gas. All of it was very careless. Though I'd been coming to Greece all my life, I'd rarely driven there, let alone traversed borders alone, driving hours at a time. In fact, I can count the number of times I've driven in Greece on one hand. Once a few years earlier, on the island with my cousin; another time throughout northern Greece into Bulgaria. And one disaster when I was nineteen, driving my boyfriend's car, on an island, because he and another friend had gotten too drunk. A manual transmission, which I'd only learned to drive that spring, not in Greece but at the biological station in Michigan where I was taking classes. I'd learned on a classmate's car on a warm and humid night. I'd worried about the spring peepers, those tiny frogs, all over the road. Earlier, we'd had a class, counting salamanders in leaf litter, being so careful not to touch them without gloves, not to get any bug repellent on them, because their skin was so porous and delicate.

And a few checkpoints did make me uneasy, but the men at checkpoints, toll roads, and airports always make me uneasy, their guns strapped to their chests like a threat. I had heard about the roads, the steep drop-offs, the lack of guardrails, though I had also experienced this in Greece years ago. Besides, here these guards looked like children, they were children, they smiled at me and were polite, as if I were the mother of a friend. This unnerved me, I hadn't expected it. One, seeing my

Greek driver's license, gently told me his older brother lived in Athens, he was going to visit the following month. I had heard about foreigners being targeted here, crimes of opportunity, yet much of it felt like hyperbole. For a while, on the road, I'd felt like I was being followed, but it was just some cognitive distortion. Most of the guards were fine. A bit aloof. A few were even kind.

So there was nothing ominous or menacing, yet for me the threat of violence knew no national lines, but violence itself was bordered and masculine and I had been conditioned to listen for it, could detect it in the most benign of conversations and for so long had wrongly accepted it to be a part of life.

I thought of the Albanian-born novelist who writes in Greek. Our feelings about borders have to do with our passports, he writes, and I know I can never claim to fully understand this trepidation. I understood my father's shock, years ago, when I applied for Greek citizenship, his worry that I would relinquish my US one, not understanding its power. A few years earlier, the Greek government had announced they were building a wall in the sea; meanwhile, the small island of Santorini might receive up to eighteen thousand tourists per day. None of it made sense.

I couldn't get over the strangeness of borders, the hostility of nationhood coupled with the sorrow of being stateless. The arbitrary lines we draw on bodies of land. Bodies of water. Bodies of memory.

THE ROAD UNFOLDED LIKE A TREADMILL SET ON A TOO-low speed. I knew bunkers were not a myth—I had seen remains of similar ones in Thrace—but I did not expect them to dot the landscape; I imagined them now as rentals, unique experience stays, authentic bunker, experience authoritarian communism for eighty euros per night. I mean, why not. I wanted to stop and poke around but I had this incessant need, when traveling by car and a border was nearby, to always traverse it. Even the most arbitrary borders; those even more so. American border crossings from state to state meant nothing, yet I always preferred to cross over to the next state before stopping to eat, for gas, or to stay the night. There was something about stopping just before crossing that disturbed me, the same way I didn't like to go back into the house if I forgot something, a superstition Luka understood and indulged. When traveling by train through central Europe in the early 1990s I could not get over the border guards and their passport checks, the uniforms that looked, to me then, my first time traveling alone, like a World War II movie.

Then a boisterous bloom of poppy fields rose out of nowhere, a bend of road and there they were. I nearly crashed, gawking at them, and I remembered my grandfather telling me of the poppy fields in his village, and how they went to them for long naps, and I didn't understand until I was much older what he was talking about.

I stopped the car, got out, and stood among them awhile, listening to the soft wind as it moved through them. Far off in the distance, I watched two hikers switchback along the hill. I felt exhilarated. I began to take a selfie with the flowers as a backdrop, the hill with the hikers behind me, but as I watched my face in the camera I decided against it. "Take out a photo," the idiom goes in Greek. I'd leave it here. I looked through my photos for the one of Luka on the side of the road, with the poppies, but I didn't have it. I wished I had. But it remained on his phone, with him, wherever he was.

I had a mobile signal so I booked a room at a small boutique hotel in Tirana, and when I arrived several hours later, I was greeted by a watercolor rainbow of a city and a good-looking couple who gave me enough tips to keep me in the city for a week. Here, the bunkers were museums, though I was not sure if they were authentic or kitsch, and honestly, I wasn't sure what the difference was anymore. The couple seemed disappointed I only wanted to stay one night, but I told them I'd be back. I don't know why I said that.

The hotel rooftop was lively, awash in colors of terra-cotta and gold, and the friendly guests all seemed to know and recognize one another. I sat on a sunshine-yellow couch and talked with two Bulgarian travelers, who told me about the beach they'd visited near the Albanian-Greek border with the bluest water in the world, a blue that could not get more blue. One of them drew me a map, told me to avoid GPS, suggested some other roads. I folded it in my pocket. And the bartender, my age and friendly, had a nephew who attended the university where I had once taught, one of those surprising travel moments that happen more often than one would think. In the morning I woke early and had the familiar feeling of not knowing where I was, once more reaching for a body next to me, but of course there was none.

That was when I first heard the sound of breaking glass, but I was half asleep and didn't think much of it. Tavernas always threw their glass bottles into the bins after close, and it was not unusual for the recycling and garbage trucks to collect in the middle of the night, when the roads were clear and the traffic had stopped.

I slept until eleven, something I hadn't done since I was in my twenties. I woke itchy from the mosquito bites and wondered about ticks from when I'd stood in the field, and then I thought about bedbugs, and then I jumped out of bed and stripped down to have a good look.

As if planned, that's when the housekeeper opened the door. I'm still here, I said. I held a towel that had been folded on the edge of the bed around me and told her I was sorry, I asked for a late checkout. You would imagine, after this, she'd say okay, even if reluctantly, and close the door.

Instead, she came inside. She took a good look at me, up and down, and the way I'd stripped the sheets back to inspect the mattress. My legs were covered in mosquito bites.

Why are you barefoot? she asked. This was her question, her voice frenzied, as if the floor, which appeared perfectly clean, were contaminated. I remembered the way my grandmother would freak out if I didn't wear slippers in the house, and I remembered the equal parts rebellion and discomfort I felt in my college dorm room when I traipsed around barefoot with impunity. I slid my feet into my flip-flops and she calmed down; she didn't seem to mind the towel. She began asking me questions about myself, my family, my origins, a lot for a short, naked conversation, but soon she was sitting on the edge of the bed. She told me about her kid, who had a full scholarship to an American university; she seemed concerned that the States were a negative influence, as if I, with my Americanness, had forced a certain worldview on her child.

Do you think he'll be safe there? she asked. Shootings, she said, and trailed off.

What to say to such a question, how could I assuage a fear I often had myself?

I think so, I said.

She smiled, almost, and said, Well. She stretched her arms out in front of her, examining them. I felt a moment of tenderness for her. But finally, I said, Look, I have to get dressed and get ready to go.

She stood up off the bed and looked incredulous, as if I were lying to her, and shut the door firmly.

After packing up, I went to the rooftop, where breakfast was served, to have a coffee and thank the owners. Young travelers and families spread out at long tables. I didn't want to make morning conversation, but I ate some yogurt and a peach and quickly drank a coffee.

The young couple who owned the place, smiling and chatty, both with dark brown curls and big smiles, didn't like this, it wasn't enough to eat, the hotel had gotten rave reviews for their beautiful breakfasts. So they made me an iced coffee and gave me a bag filled with some small cheese pies for the road and reminded me the name of Tirana came from the Greek word "tiros," meaning "dairy."

Then the woman handed me a small paper bag filled with cherries. Her husband, relaxed and lanky, told me to be careful and taught me a greeting that I learned later meant "May your life be long."

HAVE I EVER TAKEN A ROAD TRIP WHOSE HALFWAY POINT has not made me question what I have done? The only way out was through, though, and I was happy for the sea air, the windows lowered, the sense of driving those sea cliffs and then those straight passages of road. But had someone said, Here, leave the car, we'll fly you to Athens on this magic carpet, I would have taken it.

The Bulgarian travelers had drawn me a map to get to the beach, telling me where GPS would work and when it would lead me astray. They warned me it would be hard on my car and asked if I had a Jeep, which Luka's little car was definitely not. I decided against it.

I'd stayed in the port town on the other side of the border years ago. From there you could go to all the Ionian islands. We'd been running late for the ferry, as usual, and missed the final route for the night. The sun was low but still bright, one of my favorite times at the port. We took the slow boat the next morning, a five-hour ride, but I didn't mind. I loved this in-betweenness, the sense of the experience and also the movement. Sitting on the top deck and watching the gulls swoop down for bites of the small packets of cream crackers we'd purchased at the snack bar. We stretched out with our backpacks on the benches. Everything I needed was with me: a pair of jeans, a pair of shorts, two T-shirts, a dress.

But when I try to find the other half of the "we," I draw a blank. Or had I in fact been alone?

As a young person, I often took overnight ferries. No hotel room was necessary, and I'm surprised that I also traveled alone this way, trusting myself to the goodness of strangers, sleeping on a hard, slatted white bench with all my belongings at my feet. I had little with me those days, of course, a passport strapped around my neck, beneath my clothes. No phone, no laptop, one book at a time; when I'd finished one I'd give it away and find another.

And then the summer after college when my friend Kostis and I worked at a bar on that island, filled with British and American expats and travelers. It was an American bar, and some people did tip drunkenly well, despite the common perception, whereas others tipped nothing at all. Those who tipped us did so with great inebriated display. Vacation mentality. In my years waiting tables, both in Greece and in the States, I was often tipped hugely and egregiously. More often than not it felt deeply patronizing, as though the grand tip carried unspoken expectations, a sort of mastery over me, and since then I've been cognizant of the power that runs beneath large displays of generosity.

We were paid in cash at the end of each two-week period; we ate every night for free. We lived in an old, shabby hotel where other seasonal workers lived. Greece was still on the drachma. It was then that I learned that the word "drachma" meant "to grab a handful," something I thought of when I came home with cash. A few days a week I babysat, parents finding me by word of mouth. All this seemed more fun and sophisticated than our Ionian village where everyone knew where we came from, knew the houses our parents and grandparents had grown up in, knew what time we came home at night, knew the people we loved who didn't love us back.

When I finally crossed over the border into Greece, I felt calmer. A sort of transformation. Partly the comfort of a language

I knew but also simply a sense of arrival. Yet I have always felt at ease in that space where borders cast their shadows, those gradients. It's that stark dividing line that feels violent.

I got out of the car to stretch my legs. A hawk soared above, or maybe a falcon. I'd learned the difference from the novel but had already forgotten, even though I'd written those words. Common names were only just that, and interchangeable, not the essence of the thing but compounded from it.

Where had they all gone, these people who had seemed so real?

WHAT HAPPENED NEXT WAS I STOPPED FOR THE RESTROOM and to fill up my tank. I usually loved the little stops and breaks of a road trip, but I was feeling impatient. The gas station had sparkling floors and a clean bathroom, which was always a relief. Most of the roadside places I'd stopped at had seemed fine, definitely better than some of the dumps I'd encountered in the US. Here, you could always get a decent espresso and something to eat and a clean-enough bathroom, even if you had to bring in your own toilet paper. Many of the stops showcased local specialties, whether a specific kind of pastry or homemade chicken soup or pastitsio. Boxes of loukoumi from the local confectioneries. And a friend always raved about the good Turkish food at the truck stops across Bulgaria and Romania, and once, driving to the Black Sea for a conference, I'd stopped at one and it was delicious. All these years coming to Greece and I'd had so little experience driving across the country: I moved from Athens to islands, or Athens to my father's town and then up and down the Ionian coast.

This gas station was more of a minimarket, so I bought a Coke and some chips and got back in the car, deciding then to head to the town of Mesopotamos—"between rivers"—to visit the ruins of the oracle of the dead, where people once came, first to cleanse themselves and then to enter underground tunnels where they would see the shadowy shapes of the underworld. Mythologies tended to erase the modern-day world from its landscape, but I was interested particularly in the way they coexisted. Those sorrowful waters resounding on the rocks.

Sorrow keeps breaking in.

As I was pulling away, though, about to turn onto the road that led to the highway, I was hit with the fragrant smell of grilled meat. I was not full of sorrow. I was full of hunger. Instead of turning back onto the main road I went the other way, down a short dirt road lined with bushes and trees. I was surprised to find a large old building about fifty meters behind the gas station, with its own parking lot filled with trucks and cars, and what looked like an old hotel behind it. I tended to avoid such places when alone; I'd heard stories, not of hotels but of illegal brothels, human trafficking.

But it was crowded and I was curious. I followed a group of travelers, cheerful thirtysomethings, and behind them two middle-aged men. Once inside, the young travelers stopped to look at the display case, filled with raw-meat souvlaki kebabs and sliced-up eggplant and salads, talking about what they would order, obviously regulars, or at least not first-time customers.

I sat at a table in the corner of a room, a large screened-in terrace, and a kind-eyed woman took my order while flies swarmed around a nearby table where the customers had just gotten their food. Her brown eyes were clear and large. I thought again of that feeling I had of waking up in a box, the way the table I'd chosen was in the corner, screened in, though there were holes in the screens and the flies flew in and out, in and out.

I could smell the smell of shit, human shit, as if maybe someone had not bothered to go inside and had just relieved themselves near the back of the restaurant. The waitress brought me a lemonade as I was cleaning off the sticky table with the antibacterial wipes I kept in my bag.

She immediately returned with a beautiful flatbread, enough to feed a table of four, covered in sesame and little pats of butter, and I tried to ignore the flies. I slid the windows shut to block the smell from outside, thinking it might help. It didn't, and instead the little corner in which I sat grew hot.

I could tell by the way the travelers nearby were devouring the bread, tearing off large pieces and shoving them into their mouths at great speed, as if it might be taken away, that the bread was delicious, and it was. And then she brought me a salad and some baked eggplant, both of which looked wonderful too. But the air was muggy and stagnant and I opened the window again, feeling trapped in that corner even though the restaurant was large and spacious. I could feel the small of my back grow hot and sweaty.

The young travelers sat near me, going on about the food, the platters of hot steaming food in front of them, fresh off the grill. They were speaking English but in the manner of its being simply a shared tongue.

I felt dizzy, as I had that night after the play, more than a month ago. I don't know why I stayed—hungry, weary from the driving, deranged from the last several weeks, months. Maybe travel had numbed my sense of judgment. If I'd walked into a truck stop in the middle of the US that had sticky tables and flies everywhere—many of them, after all—I would have held my breath and left.

I drank my glass of water and had just washed my hands before sitting down but had the urge to wash them again, so I got up. Like I always do, I turned the wrong way out of the bathroom and got turned around, looking at a side courtyard where two men smoked cigarettes. I walked past them, to see what was behind the building. They gave me a quizzical look.

Back inside, the kitchen had grown busy. While I was in the bathroom a small tourist bus had arrived, forty pensioners streaming in, sitting down at the tables. Was I the only one who could smell the stench from outside, see the layers of filth, see the giant flies everywhere?

I didn't want to sit back down. I needed air. The server kept her eye on me, like I was doing something wrong. I looked at her and then at my feet and that was when I noticed an older man sitting on a stoop a meter away from me, an array of knives spread out in front of him on a small colorful rug, waiting for an interested customer. His mustache was huge and white, and he looked like a stock photo: Cretan man. Smiling fisherman. Somehow I hadn't noticed him before. He smiled at me with his eyes, and I felt calmer. I greeted him politely and he nodded and kept smiling but said nothing. Not far from where he sat, a swoop of swallows dove for something, gathering on the roof of what seemed to have once been an outdoor eating area, though now a storage area. I sat on a red chair next to a stack of boxes. I wanted a shower.

An American family approached—I could tell not by their clothing or shoes, as many would assume, but by that particular mix of entitlement and hesitation, staring up at menus to order coffee as if they'd never done this before in their lives. One of their daughters, college age, cheerfully coughed over everyone. Her father kept telling her to cover her mouth, but in a playful way.

The woman working at the restaurant followed me out; at first I thought she worried I was not going to pay, but she brought me a bottle of soda water, thought maybe I was sick. I thanked her and asked for the bill.

She asked if I was a journalist, and I said no, why did she ask, but she just gave a shake of her head. I wondered if she had seen or known Luka's car? Had she been expecting him? Had I been a journalist, or said I was, what was she ready to reveal to me, or hide? I was overthinking it. Maybe I was behaving like a journalist, whatever that meant.

There was such a kindness in that moment, the offering of the soda. She asked if maybe I was pregnant, which made me laugh. I was fifty years old, I told her, and she made a big show of disbelief.

Then who are you? she asked.

I'm nobody.

You don't have a name? But then her expression changed, and she placed her hand on my forehead, checking for fever I suppose. In a crowd of men walking toward the bathroom I thought I saw that ferryman again. She somehow understood my body was reacting to something, but to what? As if my body knew something I did not. I was only reacting to some sticky tables and some uncontrollable flies. Yet there was something off about this place, it seemed to be at an angle to everything else, and it gave off an eeriness. I saw something familiar in her eyes, something of the ungovernable. We had a shared moment of dread or maybe alarm, as though we had suddenly both seen something, recollected something disturbing or dangerous, the histories that lived in our own bodies, these landscapes.

And then whatever I thought I saw was gone: She was just a woman working a long shift who wanted to make sure I was okay.

I drank the entire soda while she was there and she brought me another. She cut the bread into several pieces and handed it to me in a takeout box. The sodas were not on the bill when I paid, and I mentioned this, and she waved her hand.

Had she hoped for me to be a journalist? Had she been waiting for me, for Luka? Had I failed her? Was there something she wished to tell me, quietly, out there in the strange space of the entryway, with the knife guy and the swooping swallows and dusty stacks of boxes? As I walked to my car I thought I heard a sudden wail, an outburst, a cry, decidedly human, and I started to think all these sounds were coming from another space that I walked through, the sound somehow breaking through.

I was relieved to be back on the road.

NOT FAR AFTER THE RESTAURANT, A TRAFFIC SLOWDOWN appeared out of nowhere. No warnings, no cops slowing things down, though there was a police car on the side of a road, responding to an accident. I had to slam the brakes not to fly into the cars ahead, and just as I screeched to a stop, another screech of tires behind me, a loud crash. More tires.

Oh my god, someone shouted, but before it I heard a primordial sound from elsewhere, or maybe from deep inside me. A deeply bodied utterance rising up. Before language, after all, we still had voices. What came before voice, before lyric? I wanted to crawl out of my skin and out of the car, leaving it there in the road.

And then there was a police officer looking into my window, asking if I was okay, and the first thing I thought was, or maybe I said it: I want to wash my hands.

He gave me that familiar look, as though I were translucent, or somehow not a living being, somehow not worthy of the space my body occupied, of no service to anyone. But in the end he was very kind, so maybe I imagined it.

I gave him my information, and he explained to me the process of filing the report; why they couldn't just file the report I don't know. I knew I would not remember all the details, particularly because the police officer told me very quickly in Greek, a script he probably repeated all day long. The man who'd hit my car was sharply dressed, pressed jeans and a pressed shirt, and he looked skittish and suspicious when talking to the cops. Bald and with large eyes, a beard, dark-framed glasses. He apologized to me graciously, he'd tried to stop but the curve in the road had not allowed him to see, and why weren't the cops parked farther down, slowing down traffic?

The front end of his car was completely crumpled, whereas mine was barely damaged at all. I felt a pain in my neck, subtle but present.

Why are there so few novels about women without children? the officer asked me.

What?

I offered him the box of bread, which he peered into and tore some off, taking a bite. He looked into the back, at the tote bag of fruits I'd bought at a roadside stand, the rest of my disheveled belongings. Do you think you are hurt, he said, do you need an ambulance?

Oh, I said. No. I think I'm okay. I drew my hand to my neck.

He told me to get out of the car, but don't they say that this is what you should never do, never stand there on the side of the road?

I recalled the ferryman and an imagined conversation between us.

You went about it all wrong, the ferryman said, over and over.

I am a fake woman, I now said to the officer.

Ma'am, he said, but in Greek. Kyria, what do you mean?

I recalled that incident on the ferry, the way the man charged toward me afterward in his car. He was faceless, a whir of features. Again I smelled the sea close by, but here the road had taken me into the interior: Yet there it was, that dizzying smell of diesel and salt, the strong smell of grilled meats, the wet and dank smell of the fish market, I smelled these things all at once.

I instinctively brought my hand to my chest. It was then I noticed that the small evil-eye pendant I always wore around my neck was gone. When had I last seen it?

I could have lost it anywhere. It was probably floating somewhere in the sea.

THOUGH IT WAS NOT RAINING IN CENTRAL GREECE, I expected it to be; the year before, the region had received more rain in two days than it normally rained in a year—the most rain that had ever been recorded, and the damage was still everywhere. It had been the worst flooding in centuries, the worst flooding since flooding had been recorded. And all this after the summer's fires, which had also been the worst in history, and the tourist numbers that summer were the highest as well. The summers would only get hotter. The drive had been clear and dry, the land now parched, a cycle of extremes.

Despite my accident, the car seemed drivable enough—what did I know of cars?—but back behind the wheel I felt a fog over me, as though I were driving at night, with the headlights the only thing letting me know I was there.

I did not think, then, I had a concussion. When you have a concussion I don't think you realize it, which is why they tell those around you to keep a close eye. But no one was around me. I didn't get sick and I didn't throw up and my eyesight felt okay. I remembered the crash, which seemed a good sign—those white bars of tape over my memory, over my vision, did not return.

Yet overall I had a feeling of slowness, of being off. My movements felt jerky and my neck was sore. I knew the old advice had been to stay awake but that now it was recommended to rest. Maybe I should stop. Another crossing, and then.

WHEN I CROSSED OVER INTO THE PELOPONNESUS, WHICH in my imagined cartography I always saw as one big island created with the construction of the Corinth Canal, I decided to drive to the umbrella pines that stretched out to the sea, and to take the coastal road all the rest of the way. The weather turned moody. For a few minutes when I stopped for a coffee I looked through my phone for pictures to see when I had last worn my necklace, but I had captured only sloping hills, rocky coves, fields of flowers. Narrow, medieval-looking alleyways. Luka walking ahead of me through the old town, or on a hike through lavender fields, through olive groves. A frieze on a building, the face of a masked woman. A building with a terra-cotta sculpture of Apollo atop it.

Many photos were of the sea each morning before my swim, never the same. There was only one selfie, but the suit I wore had a high halter neck and obscured my jewelry. I was not wearing the necklace in the photos from the translators' residency; in one group photo I was in a V-neck dress and my neckline was bare. Another photo of my friend and me, that she'd sent, on the ferry; in this photo I could see the glint of the chain.

No matter.

I loved those trees, the small churches their clusters created and the contrast of the slabs of rock behind them. Like clouds that rose over a mountain before a storm. On the side of the road I drank from a faucet that tapped water from the healing springs, and I felt a knot in my throat. I sang a few lines of a folk song, about a woman going to fetch some water, allowed it to release from deep in my body and attach to something larger.

I had been dreaming of this forest, thinking of it, imagining all that shade where there was otherwise none. At first the forest felt spectral, like the ghost forests of the Atlantic, but as I drove through, it felt raucous and alive. At the beginning of the nineteenth century, Greece had been 40 percent forest; now it was only 18 percent. I tried to picture this older landscape but could not; the forests here always felt surprising to me amid the craggy rock and scrubby plants. I'd read once, somewhere, about villages that cropped up along rivers and then later disappeared entirely.

I parked the car in a small gravelly patch. I walked into the forest to be seen. Walking those trails gave me the same relief as strolling my grandparents' olive grove, produced the comforting sensation of falling asleep while a person you loved was nearby, reading or watching television. I was not sad as much as perplexed, somehow hollowed out and heavy all at once.

I hiked until the mosquitoes became too much. Then it began to drizzle. I was overcome with a need to sleep.

There was a small hotel, and though I was less than three hours away, I checked in. Aside from the people who worked at the nearby taverna, and a lone couple at the other end, near the turn of the cove, I had the beach to myself. I wanted to swim, despite the light rain, but didn't trust my abilities after the accident, so I took a long hot shower.

The hotel café was on the ground floor, facing the water, with a patio covered by an awning and large tables for big groups. I had barely eaten at the strange truck stop and could not remember when I'd eaten before. I wanted to confirm my body, make sure I was still here. When I spoke to the waiter, I was surprised to hear my voice rising out of my body, mellifluous and pained and deep. As if I had somehow doubted it. The waiter was kind and treated me delicately. What did he see in my face?

An American man was talking about Orpheus and his caves and the underworld to a group of fresh-faced students with bedhead, I guessed part of a semester abroad program, but then he switched to talk about the geology of the region. I'd forgotten I'd originally been heading to the oracle, and now it felt like an afterthought, a random destination I didn't really want to reach.

The taverna was welcoming and cozy and the music was eclectic. First, the Greek song "The Night Smells like Jasmine," a new cover of it. Then "Dance Me to the End of Love," which I'd danced to with Luka, and which I had not heard, before then, in decades. I ate a plate of spaghetti with mizithra and a salad of cucumbers and bright red tomatoes, remembering reading the Balkan scholar: "Tomatoes are redder by the sea."

IN THE MORNING THE SUN RETURNED LIKE A VICTOR AND I drank coffee on my hotel balcony and watched the swallows swoop, skimming the surface of the water and then flying back up. In the air they looked like bats and on the surface of the water like flying fish. Down on the deserted beach I spotted a large brown rock near the water next to another flat one; it looked like a body curled up, knees close to chest, facing the east. Something swirled farther in the distance, an eddy, a pile of playful dolphins, a trompe l'oeil.

I would swim before taking off. I pulled on the swim cap Neda had given me, at first unable to decide if I wanted to use it or preserve it. The air felt still a bit cool but the water warm. Though I was not sure from where—there is always a church—I heard the sounds of the morning's liturgy broadcast over loudspeakers. I knew there was a baptism taking place because the kid's screams were broadcast too.

My brother was baptized twice: first in the Ukrainian Catholic church on Martin Street in Detroit, and again at the Agios Nikolaos Greek Orthodox cathedral in Halandri. With a boy, you cannot celebrate them enough. I was baptized once, and not in Greece; the occasion of my birth was not celebratory enough to warrant this special trip. Besides, my cousin Haris, born to my father's sister two days before me, was the one to celebrate. My brother is a Konstantinos, one of the important names, while I am one of the lesser saints.

But fifty years later I swam to the soundtrack of a baptism, I swam to the soundtrack of salvation and fear. The usual: Do you reject Satan, do you reject evil. There was seaweed and those white little plants that look like buttercups. No, not plants: coral, animal. They matched Neda's swim cap.

Out of nowhere the sea grew rough, as if to remind me of its power, and it was then I felt strange, was able to articulate to myself: I am mildly concussed. The waiter probably saw that I looked unwell. But it was not until my sunglasses bobbed past me, and then an espadrille, that I felt completely removed from myself. The water turned opaque, silty. I realized the tide had quickly come in and swept some of my things away.

I collected the shoe and the glasses and made my way to the shore. Luckily, the rest of my things remained dry atop a rock.

The baptism was ending. I could hear the priest, was it Holy Communion? It had been so long since I'd attended a baptism and I could not remember its components. At the sea's edge I held my captured shoe upside down to drain it. Another woman stood on the rocks, about to go in.

So sudden, she said. But where did these waves come from? There was not even a boat.

I know, I answered her. Bizarre.

"But then perhaps that is what Cavafy means," writes Olivia Laing, "that Ithacas exist merely to keep us moving and will dematerialize like a rainbow when the journey is complete."

The road to my Messenian town was lined with olive groves, and pink-blooming oleander hugged the shore. The Ionian waved to me, calm and blue and green.

What is home but a mirror, and not always a clear one? Still, I was allowing for pause and digression, but it was time to resume. I never believed in one singular Ithaca, but many. All these Ithacas.

Near the shore the rising tide sweeps onto land, but in the open sea it swells to the moon.

I ARRIVED IN MESSENIA THAT EVENING, DRIVING UP THE town's winding road made only for the initiated. The ground, in patches, was black, from fires several years before. The last time I was here, the trees, though charred, still stood. The previous summer, I'd heard they'd begun to fall, and now the land looked far more brutal than it seemed even after the fire. It took three years to really see just how badly the land, which now refused to hide its trauma, was affected.

Time passes, and the damage shows itself.

But little saplings also begin to grow. Pine forests are adapted to fire, and the root systems of olive trees regenerate, even if the branches are destroyed.

Along the coast, a misty fog settled over the sea. For a moment I lost my bearings, thought I had taken the road too far. But then, as if the road unfolded in front of me as I remembered it, I was overcome with familiarity, and there was the entrance to the narrow driveway, the two round lights that glowed at either side of the old gate.

On the high edge of the old town with the Ionian in the distance was the old house, built atop an even older foundation, something from centuries before. It was not like the shiny and new places you'd find on rental websites, yet a certain sort of renter preferred the opposite of what was found in those sanitized photos. The house did have an old charm to it, if you were the sort of person who liked this sort of thing: creamy yellow exterior, flat roof, high ceilings and crumbling plaster and a tangle of vines in the garden.

Even when I was young and staying there with my grandparents, it was always in various stages of disrepair: a bucket to stop a leak, some scaffolding over a window, a plug coming out of the wall. There was always a small crew of men repairing something: the front steps, or the outdoor winding staircase that seemed to corkscrew up forever before it reached the roof.

I had stopped at the grocery and picked up a few essentials, and I brought the bags inside, leaving them in the small foyer; I removed my shoes. I was struck by the peculiarity of time and travel, the crossing of borders, the way things appeared and then vanished.

I started some laundry, as if I'd arrived home from any old trip. Was this home now. I placed Luka's two plants on the balcony and was happy I'd given one to Neda. The night was still and warm and quiet and I was here again, a place I often went when things felt uncertain, or ended, or when a phase of my life felt as though it was drawing to a close. A re-turn. I felt a thrumming inside me again, that opening of my chest.

I sat on the couch and closed my eyes. A soft breeze blew through the curtains. The only sound in the house was the whir and pause of the washing machine. Otherwise, all was quiet, but I called out, Hello? I don't know to whom.

Maybe the translation of *Occupation* made me expect a surprise—a friend, a beloved, someone who'd taken up residence here. But there was no friend staying here as he pursued a woman; there were neither squatters nor suitors destroying the home while a spouse nervously awaited my return. No one unraveling their weaving or waiting with torches in twilight.

All those people: They existed, just not in the house. I'd find them, eventually.

But first. I turned on the heater for the hot water and waited to take a shower.

The mundanity, the commonplace, rattled me. The old marble stairs and the particular scent of the entryway. Something bloomed outside, fragrant and heady. But it was the *after* that really struck me, that everything we experienced was both static and forever dynamic. I took down the gauzy kitchen curtains to wash in the next load and let the evening light pour into the house, letting the outside in. The particular smell of the laundry detergent, so familiar, now filled the place. I opened a beer and stood in the middle of the kitchen and cried. *Where am I now?* When had I last cried? I had felt myself holding something in, and now it all poured out of me, every last bit. I missed something, someone. I missed everything.

I felt better after that lament, though, and I sipped my beer and walked around, peering into rooms. The house felt still. The French couple had decided to leave rather abruptly but it didn't have the feel of having been hastily evacuated. It was the opposite of haunted. It was unhaunted, uninhabited.

Memory often rewinds itself too far, and I had forgotten the small things I'd done over the years to update the place: new counters in the kitchen, a shower that did not soak the entire bathroom, a new coffeemaker. I had bought new mattresses, the old ones had been terrible, and I'd hired some roofers and applied a fresh coat of paint, preserving the light blue of one of the bedrooms, which my father claimed had first been pink for my aunt and then blue for him. The rest a creamy white. Much of the original furniture remained: the heavy dressers and bureaus, the kitchen table and chairs. At the old antique shop on the edge of town I had found a small writing desk for the den.

Upstairs, I found my clothes in one of the drawers, my things in one closet, and it all nearly startled me. The linen closet held a stack of old embroidered cloths, which my grandmother would have draped over every surface. They drove me nuts but I felt a wash of tenderness toward her now. I climbed the winding, narrow staircase to the roof and looked out over the town, the old harbor, the sea. The rooftop of the house in the distance, a mirror to mine, recently sold; there were no lights shining, but I could make out one lone chair.

Later, I sat on my balcony and listened for sounds from the other balcony, or the waft of cigarette smoke, or the muffled sound of a television, but the house was still. I looked out over all those rooftops, those terra-cotta tiles; I could see stars.

I felt my body opening up. In the distance, the call of an owl. A sudden shush of leaves, a thump. Olives falling from the trees.

How small it all felt. How vast.

I knew in the desk in the den there was always a pack of cigarettes, and though I'd quit years ago, I stood outside and lit a cigarette. It only took two puffs before I began to feel sick, so I put it out.

In the dark, the cigarette glowed, like a fire lit by a survivor. But who would see this light, this small dot among the infinite stars?

THE NEXT MORNING, THE CALL OF A FALCON WOKE ME. I watched him awhile, swooping and sailing, cleaving the waves. I noticed a text from Marta that I'd missed a few days before, wondering how I was doing. I only vaguely recalled seeing it when it arrived. I went through my message log and saw that Alexandra and Ioanna had also sent notes, wondering if I was in Athens. I'd get in touch with all of them soon, once I settled in.

I stopped at the bakery, drank a coffee and ate some breakfast, and then drove to the next town over, where the turtles return to mate and lay their eggs each year, the tiny turtles hatching and making their way back into the sea. I swam for a languorous hour and emerged from the water exhausted and happy.

Nearby were sandy dunes and crystal lakes and a sea like a long marriage, spots of light and spots of dark and an expanse of depth and breadth; the scraggly coastal forest stretched out to it, like umbrellas sloping to the sea. From this vista the pines seemed to walk right into the water, where they became shadowy, dusky kelp, but of course it happened the other way around. The kelp forest lived as a land dweller while remaining rooted on that seafloor.

Here, the waters are interior. Years ago, on a plane from Chicago to Athens, I nervously watched the flight tracker, zooming us over the Mediterranean, and from that perspective, I could really see the Mediterranean as an interior sea, a sea of kinship, surrounded by the lands that share its name. In this way its borders erase. This is not a vast sea but an intimate one.

I REALIZE I NEVER RECOUNTED THAT PARTICULAR DAY with Luka in the olive groves, when I was still at the translators' residency, near the old town. The small bright green lamps along the water, like miniature lighthouses, that gave the place its name. Luka and I had not taken bikes, as he'd first suggested—and after I saw how far it was, I was grateful—but a water taxi that ran between the towns.

I love the sea and I love a big ship but it's rare I agree to a boat ride. The only boats I can stomach are large, slow ferries. Even the large catamarans that run between islands make me queasy. As I expected, I spent the ride bent over the side of the boat, but when we disembarked I felt better, the world felt more glimmery and colorful. Everything shimmered around the edges; my hands had webbed fingers, my feet felt part of the sand; and at the horizon in the distance was a flash of red.

Luka and I took a long hike through the olive trees. He was charmingly obsessed with the oldest organisms on the planet: They have watched us do unfathomable things. A bristlecone pine tree in eastern California, an olive tree in Palestine, a sea grass meadow off the coast of Spain, a fig tree in Sri Lanka. He rattled them off like a litany and my chest felt so wide open, I kept thinking, I have been cracked open.

After, we walked to the old town and wandered the old walls and the fortified palace built for Saint Rocco. It was the middle of the day and the town was quiet. I was perplexed by an old mesh bag in the dirt, filled with a dozen baguettes, and Luka told me that Rocco was banished to the woods when he had the plague. The only one who'd communicate with him at all was a faithful dog, who brought him bread.

So the bread is some sort of offering, I said.

Could be, he said, as if my explanation was far too rational.

We sat in a traditional tavern, which were lacking on the other side of the island: Everything was cafés and bistros and brunch. We ordered beers and fried calamari and I remember us both as very relaxed. Luka poured the beer into our glasses and declared that we'd take a taxi back, so I wouldn't get sick.

I smiled. Sounds good.

Without words we'd acknowledged something between us, I don't want to say love but maybe it was love; it was not exactly sex, not yet, but near sex. A kind of tender attention, or care, something before or beyond the self, something ancient, our bodies and their porous borders, among the living histories of the ancient settlers who'd partitioned this land for farming, whose lines of property and trees were still intact, and the town with its layers of histories built atop histories. The way such things remain, embed themselves. The fossils of sea pollen record the history of human life, thriving and failing, failing and thriving.

The ancient world of the sea and where it meets the land. The sea as the site where all the world's crises converge.

Humans have destroyed so much, yet the olive groves partitioned off by the ancient Greek settlers, on that island where I wandered with Luka, remained intact. I told Luka about my father's town, the family olive grove that they had sold, and that years later had probably been charred by wildfire. I have always been fascinated by olive trees, the adaptability of their roots. Every old olive tree is a composite—a root and its branch, a root and its branch, a root and its branch. A system.

You never talk about that place, Luka said, the place where your father was born. I mean, you talk about Athens, he said. Or the island with the river of sand.

River of sand, I never called it that, that's lovely.

The word was "tombolo," but at that moment I couldn't remember it, and certainly didn't know the word in any other language but English. I liked "river of sand." What did it mean to name things truly?

I don't know why, I said. I suppose neither of us talks about childhood.

He nodded. I had a great childhood, he said. The later years were hard. You?

I shrugged. It was fine. I don't know. I was happy to leave it behind.

We were quiet.

You, Luka, are like an olive tree, I added.

THE SECOND NIGHT IN THE HOUSE, I WAS READING IN bed, quite sleepily, when I heard a knock on the back door. Rarely did anyone come to the front door unannounced, let alone the back. The house was not an easy one to pass by; a long, tall staircase led only to this house itself, unless you came by car, or scrambled up the hill on the scraggy path behind it, which was very steep and overgrown; I had never tried. In short, most visitors here were deliberate, or lost. To reach the back door, you had to squeeze through a narrow path on the side of the house, which was also now a bit overgrown. Then you'd have to climb up onto the terrace.

I lay quietly and listened. Perhaps someone the French couple knew, thinking they were still here. I went to the small front balcony, made only for standing, and listened. Whoever it was had given up and begun the descent down the front. Not the heavy-footed steps of a man, but the quick, light steps of a woman in sandals, soles slapping on her feet. Maybe a friend had heard I'd returned. Though a friend would have called my name, waited for me to come out. In fact, anyone who visited usually called to me this way, from the front. Or it could be the new owner of the house next door, wanting to introduce themselves.

In the translation I'd written, the narrator's friend is involved with a younger woman, as I mentioned, and in one scene, she comes knocking on the door, shocked to find not the man, who passed the house off as his, but the narrator herself. The narrator invites her in for coffee. Could it be that I dreamed it? I suppose so.

The next evening, before sunset, when everything had that grayish-purple hue, I walked from the house down the stairs to the landing; from there another path led to the other staircase, which led to the other house, which, from what I could tell, was currently unoccupied. For years I had thought about installing solar lights along the path that led up from the road, and now I wished I had. The French couple had mentioned the difficulty of walking back in the dark.

That was when I encountered a woman. She wore a green dress and sandals, dressed for a party. Her hair was loose and wavy and it looked like she'd been at the beach all day. Often tourists wandered up these stairs, expecting more winding streets or a vista from which to view the sunset, or maybe a hiking trail, but the stairs only led to those two homes. I had thought many times, over the years, to place a sign at the base, but that seemed needlessly proprietary. Besides, why announce I was up there? Most people wandered halfway up, realized it led to the pair of houses, and turned around.

I startled her, and I asked if I could help her, and she said no, no, she had taken a wrong turn. She spoke Greek but her accent was faintly American, like mine. Had we met before? I didn't ask.

It's just me up there, I said, gesturing to the staircase.

She looked up, as if I stood there, literally.

Maybe you meant to go this way, I offered. I swept my hand up toward the path. It leads to a house.

The woman peered at the path, took a few steps to it, and then shook her head. No, she said. I took a wrong turn.

So we walked along to the town silently, the flap of our sandals on the rock. As we turned a corner, we had a view of a rooftop party below us, like the time I'd seen Luka, that first encounter when he called down to me. A pop song was blaring from speakers on the rooftop, decibels louder than anything else, drowning it all out: the call of voices from the market below, the music from the cafés, the kids who played in the square. Even the incessant motorbikes. What a different perspective, from here. I felt sorry for the surrounding homes, probably still new to the idea of the in-and-out of expensive rentals. An older woman peered over one balcony while another woman on the next told her to put on a nice dress and join the party. The two of them laughed.

I heard the rise and questioning of American English and the singsong properness of British English and felt a strange sense of dissonance, like something had been superimposed upon the old town like a clear plastic overlay. I kept going.

As I walked away, I spotted a man at the edge of the party, standing in a way that made him seem like the host. From where I stood on the stairway, we were eye to eye, though the rest of the party wouldn't have seen me, such was the nature of that terrace and the staircase that traversed the hill. He raised his hand in a wave, but he was waving at the woman, who waved back at him before turning to thank me. I watched her look out at the party, and as if she'd changed her mind, disappear down the staircase and around a corner. I followed her down, out of their range of sight, and they mine, and I had a drink in the café beneath the castle, where I had a gorgeous view of the entire town and the glimmering evening sea.

As for the woman, I didn't see her again.

A few days later I walked that path down to see if anything was happening on the rooftop, to see if it had become a place with perpetual parties, rentals. The two women who'd joked about dressing up and joining the party were on their balconies, chatting; one of them was taking down her laundry, and the other was peering over the edge. They waved at me, as though they recognized me, and I wondered if they remembered me traipsing down these stairs as a child, as a teen, an American girl visiting her grandparents for the summer. Otherwise, the evening was hushed and still, and I think this recollection was a mix, my translation and my life and maybe something of Luka's novel too. I am not sure.

I felt impatient for the sun to set.

AND THEN LUKA CALLED TO TELL ME ABOUT SOME CAVES. We had not spoken since—since.

I have never been inside a cave: not in the Adriatic or Ionian or Aegean, not the sea caves or the ones carved into the hills. He'd wanted to go, when we were at Ivan's, but I'd told him I was too claustrophobic. The thought of swimming into a cave made me shiver with fear.

Years before, I'd gone with my aunt, who was a tour guide, on a trip from Athens to Egypt, and the panic I'd felt crawling into the tombs was enough for a lifetime. Luka and I had talked about the Egyptian caves, with the ancient drawings of animals, but I didn't think he was in Egypt. Which caves? I asked, thinking for a moment he might be nearby.

He didn't answer or tell me where he was, and I wasn't sure if he was ignoring my question or simply immersed in his own story. The caves went on and on, and you'd think you'd reached an end but then there would be a small hole and you knew there was something beyond it, another entrance, a cave extending deeper and further. You wouldn't believe it, he said.

I thought of how, beneath the oracle of the dead, scientists had found a chamber that was anechoic, completely without sound. I could not imagine what that meant, to have no reverberations, no resonance, to really understand silence. I remembered the long tunnel on the island, the one that went on and on and had affected Luka so markedly. These two things felt related.

I did not ask how the trip was or what he'd been writing because I knew it had not been easy for him, that something had been happening to him at the reminder of all these wars, a new war now eclipsing the last, yet he kept doing it to himself, as though compelled not to look away. This I knew from our late-night conversations. I did not ask him for any explanations; somehow, I didn't need them.

But he continued to speak. He said he'd gone down into a cave city, six, seven, eight stories down, and had his first panic attack in twenty years. As he was telling me I could sense the panic rising in his voice, coming up again.

The claustrophobia? I asked.

I don't know, he said.

You're okay now, I said, to gently remind him, and also to ask.

I know I have mentioned the way Luka would always call me when I lived in the States, late night for him, when something had gone wrong romantically. When he'd lost something, when he'd experienced disappointment, when he'd been grieving a breakup. The way he would talk and talk. I sensed a similar grief in his voice, though heavier.

There were many entrances to the underworld, along with five rivers, but I didn't say this. But then his voice calmed. He seemed less afraid and told me about the mineral deposits of caves, the way they created a record of sea level rising.

How are you? he asked, interrupting himself.

I was quiet. How could we have been so close yet so mutually indecipherable to each other? I'm okay too, I said. I waited for him to mention his car. My voice was blocked; it wouldn't rise from my throat. In the end I didn't mention it, and he didn't ask. Maybe he hadn't even been back to know. What made sense was that it had ended between us the way it began, another recursive playing out of something before, and something that might still be.

We talked for a while, about this and that but also about nothing. I knew that the next time I saw him, all this time between us would be erased.

I turned in my book, he said.
Congratulations, I told him. How do you feel about it?
You know how it is. Once the book is finished . . . ?
It no longer belongs to you, I said.

Then I asked, Will you send me a copy? I wondered if I actually wanted to read it, or let it be, framed by the borders of the page, rendered into text. To let it be, or let it appear to me. I wondered how much of me remained in those pages.

A book is framed by its physical shape, but the story goes on and on, one thing merging into the next. I imagined the cover, a figure of a woman in a navy dress on a hill overlooking the sea, or descending a staircase while looking up toward a rooftop.

Of course, he told me. Then he said, You're near the train station; he said, I hear it.

I could hear nothing but the quiet wind in the trees.
Must be something on your end, I said.
Could be, he said.

THERE WAS A BEACH I LOVED NOT FAR FROM HERE, WHERE the Neda River ran into the sea. Twenty minutes away, by car. The road up the coast was filled with the scent of curing olives, or olives pressed for oil, I wasn't sure.

Along the drive, I thought of Neda, wondering how she was.

When I arrived, I dropped my things in the sand, waded into the river. On this beach is the opposite of the tombolo; here the beach is split by water. Just before it reaches the Ionian it cuts to the side to run parallel to the shore, and the sand flanks this river on both sides, creating a second small beach between the river and the sea. It's only what it is because of the water around it; the surrounding banks shape the river, which shapes the surrounding banks.

Water returns to where it began, to where it was.

I walked up on the spit of sand between and emerged into the cool sea. The beach was near empty: one group of sunbathers on the other side of the cove, and one man and woman walking together along the shore. Farther down the beach, three men seemed to be fighting something in the water; they'd set up nets to catch some type of fish as it gushed from the river, a type of fishing that was both unethical and illegal. Or were they trying to trap turtles?

I began to approach them, and one of them looked up and saw me walking toward them. I felt watched and instead turned to the water in front of me and placed my feet in the water. I swam for a while, and when I emerged from the sea, I saw they'd given up and were leaving empty-handed. I felt smug, relieved.

I dozed on the beach and was woken by the sound of voices nearby. A group of women in their sixties or seventies had spread out their things on blankets and were now in the water; I hadn't heard them arrive. They were half swimming but mostly talking, but the brightness of the sun did not allow me to see their faces. Water carried sound. I could not hear what they were saying but heard that they spoke both Greek and French. Something in the way the sound carries is different from one language to the next, the way the stresses fall, the way the stresses fall, the way the stresses fall.

Mostly I heard laughter; I dipped into the water and swam out. When I surfaced, I could see them exiting the water and realized they were all stark naked—though they, a detail both curious and delightful, wore hand paddles, the sort swimmers use for training. One of them flapped them in the air, like wings.

The women didn't seem to notice me, but I felt calmed by their presence. As I was packing up to leave, I saw another two women coming down to meet them; they emerged from the opening at the river, came right out of that forest. Hey, gorgonas, one of the two shouted to the group on the beach—gorgonas was Greek for "mermaids"—and they greeted the pair warmly and wildly, like it had been years since they'd spoken but probably they'd been there last week too.

After they joined their friends, I walked to the base of the vegetation, from where they had emerged, where long strands of bamboo and pine swayed over the river before it turned and ran parallel to the beach. The morning light was dappled and it seemed like an entrance to another world.

I put my foot into the river there and marveled at its force. I wondered from where those two gorgonas had emerged, from where they had walked. I waded in against the current and told myself I'd return the next day, this time to the Neda Waterfalls. I'd take a long morning hike and follow the river all the way back here, where it flowed into the sea.

HERE IN GREECE, THE RIVERS RARELY HAVE A SINGLE source: They spring from the mountains at several places. In this way, the beginning is often many places at once.

THE NEDA WATERFALLS HAD BECOME SOMETHING OF A tourist attraction, though I remember the place as quiet and relatively unknown to travelers, mostly through the word of mouth of more serious hikers. It was here, near these waterfalls along the Neda River, where they say the American woman had really disappeared the previous summer: not at the Venetian fortress and not near the Castle of Giants and not in the caves and not on the outskirts of town. I'd thought of her when walking near the translation center, and when I'd arrived at the house.

I woke early the next morning and drove toward the falls, thinking of her again.

If you wanted to take a daylong hike, maybe six hours, you could walk from the farthest waterfall along the river all the way to the sea where I'd gone swimming the day before. I'd been to that waterfall a few times—Neda the nymph, one of the thousand daughters of Okeanos, became the river, but the waterfalls were formed from her braids—and still recalled the charm of it appearing, the way it asserted a presence when no one else was around.

The first time I'd come, years ago, the trail had been quiet and it felt like we'd discovered something no one else knew about, though of course many did. Somewhere nearby, in the mountains, were old TB clinics, probably still inhabited by ghosts. The last time I'd visited was in the middle of summer, and it felt more like a beach party than anything else. Dozens of people unprepared for hiking, dressed for the beach, taking photos of the waterfall. One woman in white sandals, while taking a selfie, had slipped and gashed her knee; she had to be carried away by her friends, the long path back to the car.

Along the lesser-traveled trails were some beautiful sites, gorgeous vistas, and I preferred to hike those, which was what I'd done on that last visit, to avoid the crowds. So I drove away from the falls and parked my car near the small church at whose base sprang a natural spring. Several trailheads branched from this small lot, where the spring emptied. I recalled filling my water bottles here.

The path along this section of the Neda was cleared and often ran a bit above the river itself, though sometimes it disappeared into the river's bank, or merged with the river entirely. At one such place, I thought I glimpsed a body lounging on the bank, a river goddess, outstretched sandaled feet. The light was dappled and playing tricks.

The hike was not easy, which I expected, because the terrain was not always stable. I crossed the river, I got wet, I lost the trail or maybe the trail disappeared but soon I found it again. What I did not expect was such a roaring body of water. I began the descent into a ravine, and the forest began to rise around me.

Farther up, by the falls, you needed special gear for wading the river, maybe even a helmet to protect yourself from falling stones, but I thought from this point on it would be more straightforward. I thought I'd be okay, but as I said that to myself, I felt a wave of nerves. I shouted out my name, and then repeated Echo, echo, echo, and my name, and Echo, echo, echo, sealing myself, and that moment, into the landscape. Both voice and antiphone, call and response.

The route felt more familiar than I had imagined it would. I stood next to a tree and took my hair from its bun. I stood straight like the pines. I was hot and sweating, but the water was so cool and glorious on my body. My sneakers were supposedly made for wet trails, I recalled buying them at an outdoor shop in Athens the previous summer, but the water squeaked in them as I walked along. The birds were going berserk. As I neared the coastal forest, I passed an old abandoned boat and felt a moment of recognition, like I had seen it before, conjured it in my mind. I wondered if the boat belonged to me. A weird thought, I know.

I walked slowly and carefully. Sometimes on a matted path and other times along the slippery stones of the river. On that trail I both saw myself and did not, there I was, there I am. My upper body felt muscled, like I could have thrown a rock that could sail to Italy, or back to the Dalmatian coast. I felt the muscles of these legs, so many years of movement, this body emptying itself into the forest, the sea, the forest and the sea rush in, this hair now streaked with gray, in the mirror of the sea she is alive, I am alive, I am the river Neda, she is I, this was the point. The sea like the sponge that absorbed all of me. Me, I have been colonized by coral.

The forest created sound and that sound, when I walked through it, merged with my thoughts, replaced my thoughts, spoke to me like a memory. I felt calm. This was why forests were the enchanted ones, their song an incantation, inviting us to be still. What is dimly remembered in these woods, in these bones, in the rivers and their maps? Enchantment or terror or something tumbling out, my body like a jellyfish in my own hands. Shape-shifting and self-rejuvenating and never one thing, like grief, like sex; like bread from wild yeast, like wild yeast from air.

All there is and all there was and all that ever will be.

WHEN I FELT MYSELF NEARING THE SEA, I BEGAN TO RUN down the slope, my feet almost getting out from under me, and emerged from the thicket of bamboo and pine, the place from which the two women, the gorgonas, had emerged yesterday to join their friends.

Though the trail had felt familiar, I did not recognize the beach immediately; I'd never entered it from this perspective. The beach was fairly secluded yet I felt as though I were watched, and I was, by a curious dog on the other side of the spit of sand.

Down the beach a bit were some of the gorgonas again, swimming close to the shore. Did they come every day? I assumed the dog belonged to them. I dropped my backpack in the sand and stripped off my clothes, my shoes, and crossed through the river to the small bank of sand before walking into the sea.

The dog watched me swim from the other side of the sand, on the other side of the river. I didn't swim for long, and he seemed relieved when I emerged from the water, crossed through the river again, and rejoined my things on the beach. I spread my thin blanket on the sand and drank some water. The dog settled in next to me, in the sand. I lay back and closed my eyes and fell asleep awhile. When I woke, the dog was gone.

The sun had grown hot-hot and I stood up to swim again. Was this a natural beach, as they called beaches without beach chairs and a café, and also beaches where you could feel free to lounge without clothes? Was I out of place with my bikini, should I have taken it off? No, no matter. I donned my goggles and my swim fins—"frog sandals" in Greek, a term I loved.

When learning to swim, we tend to kick like frogs, something I read and have thought about a lot, as though we, too, had recently crawled onto land from the sea. To kick back and forth is far more difficult to learn than the frog kick. I learned to swim so long ago that I have only one memory of it: struggling to puff out my belly enough to float on my back and the final joy of suddenly having it come naturally. My green swimsuit. That's all.

I entered the water, somewhat self-consciously, but except for the gorgonas, no one was there. I'd lost sight of the dog; I hoped he'd found his person.

The water was delicious, and I felt my intellect and my senses and my body merge with it. I am part of the water, I have opened up to the sea. My chest wide open again, like the feeling of young love, like the feeling of young love that ages with you, hadn't I known that too? I swam far out to where the sea grew oddly shallow again; a sandbar rose up to meet me and though I did not want to disturb it, I had not expected it, and so as not to scrape myself—this was why I did not like to skinny-dip—I carefully scrambled atop it and stood with my hands on my hips, looking out at the shore. The gorgonas, I realized, were watching me, and they waved, and I waved back. From where they stood, it must have looked like I was standing atop the water's surface.

I swam to shore, where I emerged from the water backward—easier with my fins—and walked along the bank of sand that separated the sea from the river from the beach. From afar, the gorgonas clapped. I waved and walked along that spit of sand, back and forth, letting the sun dry me off. The word for "character" is the word for "engrave," which also means "the breaking of dawn."

I took off my fins. With my toe, I etched my name into the sand, and then I erased it.

When I was dry I pulled on clothes warm from the sun, and I could feel this was my story now.

THERE WAS THE DOG AGAIN, FRIENDLY, ANXIOUSLY WATCHing me. Now I noticed his collar. He had been waiting as I dried off and then followed me as I walked along the sand. The hike along the river had seemed like a good idea, and I'd known I'd have to take a taxi back to the car, but now of course it seemed like a hassle. It would be easier to get a taxi from the grocery up the road.

The dog decided that was enough. He did not want to leave the beach. He was not coming, but he barked after me.

The grocery store was farther up the road than I had anticipated, and I felt I was walking a long time. I had eaten all the snacks I'd brought and was starving, though I had others in my car. The air was hot and I was thankful for the occasional sea breeze.

As I neared the grocery, a car slowed, a Land Rover covered in dirt, and I felt my chest racing, reminding me of when I was very young and very naive, hitching rides around the Cyclades as though I were invincible. But a woman my age hitchhiking did not attract the same sort of driver, the curious need to protect and possess. I was not viewed as vulnerable and carefree and lost.

The driver lowered the window and she, cheerful and older than I, seemed familiar, and I recognized her voice, the French one who'd called her friends gorgonas as she emerged from the river, the trees, the day before. There were two of them, in light-colored sundresses now. How long had I been walking? They must have packed up shortly after me.

They spoke to me in English. Get in, it's no problem, they said.

Did you leave your dog at the beach? one asked.

The little dog? I thought he was yours.

No, they said. But he did not want us to leave. He stood at the base of the rear tire, not letting us reverse the car, as if waiting to be invited in.

The driver thought they should go back and check on him, but her friend insisted he was fine. Just a local dog, she said. Probably lives in one of those houses on the other side of the road.

Do you need a ride somewhere? Now they spoke in Greek, in unison.

I told them I was going to call a taxi from the grocery. I explained about the hike, about where I'd left my car.

Don't call a taxi here, they said. He will never come. You'll be waiting until sundown, when he gets up from his nap. They spoke of it as though there were only one taxi driver, a lazy one at that, which very well may have been the case. I thanked them and settled into the back seat.

Most people were headed to the sea, to find relief from the heat, but we were driving to the interior. They chatted the entire way. I heard how they'd met—on a ferry forty years ago, to Paros, the island was different then, you know, they said, and I said I did. On their last day together they'd planted two tamarisk trees on their special beach, and now the trees stood proud and gave shade to all the beachgoers. The one in the passenger seat showed me a photo on her phone.

I nodded, impressed.

This is nothing, the driver said. We'll all be dead before it reaches its full size.

They continued their story.

They'd fallen out of touch soon after those young years on Paros, and it was not until the pandemic, with so much life already lived, that they'd both gone back to the island and—coincidentally—found each other. They still lived there now, they told me.

It was a beautiful coincidence, like all stories. They were here, though, for a niece's wedding, had decided to stay the week and explore.

The interior of the car, despite its travels to the beach, seemed very clean. On the floor next to me was a bag of knitting: yarns of purple and sea blue, a glimpse of something in progress. A beach bag with their hand paddles, some towels.

I directed them to the small gravel lot from where I'd begun the hike, next to the faucet that tapped the spring. The two other cars that had been there earlier were still there.

But my car—Luka's car—was gone.

Here? the driver asked.

Yes, I said. I tried to think quickly but I could tell they heard the confusion in my voice.

Which car? the other asked.

I stared at the lot.

Are you sure you're okay? the driver asked. You're sure your car isn't at the beach?

Is it one of those? the other said, pointing at the other two cars, covered in dust.

No, I said. It was right here. Dark green.

They were trying to be helpful, talking to me gently, the way I'd spoken to my father when he'd begun experiencing dementia, the way Lyuba had spoken to Neda. Maybe it was another small lot?

I'm positive, I said. Here near the fountain. I'm sure of it.

They both got out of the car with me, as though maybe we weren't looking closely enough. One of them wandered around the small church.

The car was right here, I said, standing in the spot where I'd parked. That was when I noticed, next to the other two cars and an old fig tree, two canvas bags of books and clothes and snacks. I looked around the lot, carefully, in case my eyes were playing tricks on me. But no. Luka's car was not there.

These are my things, I said.

And this: Strung over a bush, as if someone had been changing and hung it there to dry, was a long navy-blue dress. I held it up to my body, as I would in a mirror. Then I draped it around my neck like a scarf, like a snake, and leaned against one of the dusty cars, as if I were fooling anyone. The earth was bruised with overripe figs.

Strip off your clothes and leave the raft behind / for winds to take away.

I HAD TO THINK A MOMENT. I RUMMAGED THROUGH THE things the thieves had left me, as if looking for keys to an invisible vehicle.

I drank some water and the three of us ate some of the pistachios that had been in my bag. I could feel the eyes of the gorgonas watching me, waiting for me to say what they knew.

Okay, I said, meekly. My car has been stolen.

Stolen, one repeated.

Where can we take you? the driver asked. The police?

I was imagining that conversation: The car I took from my former lover and drove across several borders has been stolen. I'll just go home first, I said.

I gathered the canvas bags and clambered back into their back seat.

I told them where the house was. They were not staying far from there, it turned out. The next village over, a family home of a friend, the Greek one told me.

They didn't ask about the bags of books, the random things the thieves had left behind. I was still starving.

If they thought the navy dress slung around me was strange, they said nothing.

On the radio, a song, about a young woman with a body that drove even the priest mad—blame the woman for her body!—which they sang along to at the top of their voices, and I joined in too.

Now stop your ship and listen to our voices.

THE CHATTY GORGONAS—THEY WERE LESS LIKE GORGOnas, really, than they were birdlike sirens—were heading south to the other seaside village, but because the national road went right through my town's center, they insisted it was no problem to take me to the house. A family house? asked the Greek, and I said yes. She nodded; it needed no more explanation.

For much of my adult life, the house was both there and not there, here and gone. There were times in my life I felt very connected to it and other times I didn't give it much thought. I told this all to the gorgonas, I don't know why. We've heard stories like yours so often, one said. The one in the passenger seat turned to face me, telling me a similar story of her family, a house in Mani that stood empty yet unavailable all at once.

A house you might see in a travel magazine, the driver said.

"Twenty Mediterranean Houses You Can Buy for Under €5,000," the other added.

I laughed. But I always clicked on those headlines, I said.

Who were these people, who bought such homes, who traipsed into any old country to purchase a piece of its land for themselves? Friends told me stories of Americans buying something in the Mediterranean and immediately selling it, overwhelmed with the bureaucracy and paperwork and the very nuanced, unstraightforward ways of transactions here, stories that were told to me with a dash of smug delight. I admit I enjoyed these stories too, not because I wanted to rejoice in this failure but because we Americans so often assumed that everything could belong to us. A transaction in Greece was never simply a transaction; you had to pretend it was casual and friendly, and a dash of business thrown in as an afterthought.

It was a part of Greek life that I'd always admired yet found exhausting and confusing, the temporal performance around the exchange of money or goods.

It was shameful to talk about money or business, too capitalist, too mercenary, so you sat and ate a huge lunch and drank little pitchers of raki until everyone felt okay about mentioning the business, only in the last 10 percent of the time, as if you had almost forgotten and it didn't matter that much anyway. I delighted in the way the subtext worked, and recalled the linguist who'd noted that among three groups, Americans, Greek Americans, and Greeks, it was the latter who interpreted the most nuance in a request, a phrase, with the Greek Americans right in the middle. What is trafficked through language depends on your perspective.

The gorgonas parked in the center of town, a long way from the house, and to walk from there was all uphill, snaking through the roads or occasionally climbing up flights of stone stairs. First, the gorgonas stopped at the grocery on the main street. Across the street, the owners of the Pharos taverna sat at a table together, watching soccer.

I walked through the narrow grocery aisles, picking up a few things. It was not easy to come and go unnoticed in this town, and people knew one another's family history going back for generations. The cashier did a double take, and another woman ahead of us in line looked me over, up and down, up and down, as if startled to see me. I don't know. Maybe I imagined it. When I was a kid, people were always stopping me to marvel at my eyes and my brow, saying they were the same as my father's and his father's too.

Back in the parking lot, the gorgonas offered to drive me up to the house.

I don't know why, but I wanted to approach the house alone, on foot, to walk through the new town, then the old town, up the hill. My first arrival had been by car, on the winding roads that switchbacked up the hill.

You live alone? the first asked.

It had taken some getting used to, that I was now living alone. I have always been comfortable with solitude, which is not a disposition but a choice, and in this retelling I'm speaking mostly of solitudes. It does not mean I dislike the company of people, I don't at all, but there are other ways to be in company and maybe that's what's been on my mind. I needed to be alone so I might soon not be. Solitude did not imply the singular.

I felt strange saying goodbye to them, remembering how long it had been since I'd been in the company of women, the relief of it, but all these women lived inside me now. Personhood and kinship to me were linked, and maybe because I believed this, I didn't mind being alone from time to time. I have always loved to be surrounded by people I love, but this is not part of this story. Something had happened that freed me, that would allow me to both start over and return.

Be well, they told me, and I told them the same.

Farther up the hill, I ran into two friends from my youth, Kostis and Katerina, who seemed startled by my presence. They recognized me right away. Their grandparents had owned the house next to the old store, but I hadn't seen either of them in probably fifteen years. Both of them lived in Athens now. Kostis had been my first love, and there had been no bad energy between us, not then, not ever. We'd been very young. Katerina was six or seven years younger; I used to babysit her, change her diapers, take her swimming.

It's you, Kostis said. And then he said it again. Where are you? he asked, meaning, Where have you been?

Where am I now?

You look exactly the same, Katerina said to me, and I laughed because of course it was not true.

Do you need a ride up to the house? he asked.

Where's your car? Katerina added.

It's a long story, I said. And thought: A long, recursive story. The same story in many different forms.

We also haven't been back here in a few years, Kostis said.

I nodded and smiled. I'm so happy to see you, I said, and I could feel my lower lip tremble.

He pulled me into a hug and then extended his arms to look at me. And kept looking at me.

I would recognize you anywhere, he said.

I COULD NOT SEE THE HOUSE FROM DOWN THERE, BUT I felt its gaze. I began the walk from the road up those stairs, up toward the medieval castle. There was a café up there now, open in the morning for coffee, and when there were concerts in its ampitheater you could hear them at the house. It had been a long time since I'd approached it this way, not by car from the road that wound up the hill, but walking, straight up, vertically.

The sheer cliffs and coves that flank this village prove the power of currents, of ancient river mouths, forces of tension and rocks that collided until they appeared to be one body. Forests that look like clouds stretch their roots to the sea, watching us watch them, move through them. Turtles that return and a seafloor forest named after shadows and the sirens who refuse to be just one thing.

HALFWAY UP TO THE HOUSE I STOPPED AT A SMALL OVERlook, which had two benches and some potted flowers. From there you could see the entire town, all the way to the sea, but if I looked up in the other direction I could glimpse a small part of my balcony, and the entirety of the other house. I grew up on a balcony with a view of another balcony, wasn't that a song? I sat down on the bench and the entire town unfurled below me: rooftops and terraces and rooftops, laundry hanging, music playing, the sound of someone playing the piano.

I recalled Katerina saying, when I ran into her and Kostis, that the other house had recently fallen to foreign hands, as if a battle in a war. Many British people were buying homes here, particularly after Brexit, hoping to get a golden visa. Soon there will be no more locals, Katerina had lamented. But it was less a xenophobic statement than an anti-capitalist, anti-globalist one: the wealthy French and Germans and British, Americans and Israelis and Chinese, buying up properties as if it were sport. I couldn't imagine it happening here, the local areas packed with vacation rentals, but also knew it was a matter of time.

THERE WAS AN OLD HOUSE KOSTIS AND I LIKED TO POKE around, as kids, as teens, and sometimes we'd bring Katerina and try to scare her with stories of ghosts. She was very little, though, and didn't know to be scared. She kept saying hello to people who were not there in a very matter-of-fact way that instead scared the shit out of us. We didn't go back again for a very long time. When I returned after my first summer in college, it had been torn down to unearth an old hammam, about which the Ottoman travel writer had written that it sometimes works, sometimes doesn't. Near the grounds of the old hammam, inspired by it, was a spa, with pools and baths and saunas, which boasted water bottled from a nearby healing spring that was said to be good for kidney stones.

I spent many childhood summers in this village with my grandparents. When I was having a string of headaches, my grandmother told me to go see a friend of hers who lived down the road. That's what it was like then; I marched down the little narrow road, knocked on a door, and told the woman who answered the door that my grandmother had sent me. She called to her husband, who at the time was the tallest person I had ever seen, and I don't remember what happened, some preparations, some prayers, because I remember being fascinated by their house, which seemed to me then like a cave with endless other cavelike rooms emerging from it.

Sometimes, I visit that house in my dreams, rooms within rooms, curved doorways opening out into riad-style courtyards, though I'm not sure if they were in the original house or not.

At the top of the hill, instead of turning toward the house, I followed the road toward the castle. A tiny kitten dodged out from under a car and pounced on a bird, and now it trotted toward me with the poor creature squirming in its mouth. Beyond the car was where my great-aunt Hariklia once had a small store—beans, flour, sugar, olive oil, big jugs of wine. A jar of loukoumi.

I could not remember the last time I'd walked this route. I passed a man, a luthier, in a large window, making a lyra. He waved.

I imagined I'd find the store boarded up, or turned into a trendy two-story place called—in English—Warehouse or Garden or Tea, or an H&M, but I was happy to see it was still a cheerful little store. What was once the storage basement was now a garage, and on the ground floor you walked into an open, sunny space. Modernized, sure, but it still had a sense of the old kafeneio; you could also buy coffee and coffee apparatuses, sandwiches with smoked ham and graviera and pistachio pesto, and a small selection of dairy from the family's own farm. Some barrels of olives. The downstairs showed teas and coffees and sweets, some small groceries. An update to her store, but it held its character.

There was the jar of loukoumi, and I bought several. I also bought some olives and some coffee to take with me, and a sandwich for later. I went upstairs, where my great-aunt had lived. Now it was an eating space that opened to the air.

BEYOND IT WAS THE NEW SPA, AND I WAS HAPPY TO SEE IT had not been fashioned in that day-spa manner, the simplicity that becomes cliché, the healing music and the low voices and the inoffensive yet somehow bloodless aesthetic. It was a mix between a mountain lodge, somewhere you might eat soup and drink tsipouro after a long hike, and a low-key beach bar. There were some kitschy touches but overall it retained a unique charm. Ten years ago it seemed the bars and tavernas and boutiques that sprang up were not Greek but Greek-themed, as if they existed outside this landscape instead of within it, but here there was no blue evil-eye wallpaper to be found. The spa's glass light fixtures, the grandness of the marble, the sense it was as much a part of the community as it was for visitors, seemed to resist the more common tropes.

There was a private option, but I chose the public, the more traditional way, and a woman scrubbed my back until I had no skin left, I had been inverted, and I didn't know when the last time was that I had washed my hair so thoroughly. Everything smelled like neroli, like jasmine. The woman looked like Neda, for a moment I thought it was, a bit younger, the same large eyes like almonds. I stood obediently while she scrubbed my front, and she held my butt so I wouldn't move, like you might scrub a child. I laughed out loud. The woman asked what was wrong. Oh, nothing.

I stared at the flat marble wall and down at my feet, and I thought of the woman's feet I'd thought I'd seen at the river, then my own feet. I had gone through a phase where I'd painted my toenails, yet now the practice, for me, seemed garish. There was another woman in the baths, down from me, and I focused on her feet, her toes painted like bougainvillea.

Years ago, I'd gone to some natural thermal springs on the island with the tombolo, where I began this story. Built up around the springs was a public spa, and next to that spa was a large but modest hotel. The spa was closed now, they said temporarily, though the springs still bubbled up inside it but no one could access them. I'd heard a big foreign investment company wanted to buy it and probably turn it into something flashy and expensive. Meanwhile, the locals, proud of these natural resources, had created a makeshift pool surrounded with stones, allowing the spring water to flow into the sea. At all hours you could find locals and visitors alike soaking in those warm, healing waters, waters that did not belong to anyone and were also not for sale. Once, long ago, these waters, emerging red from the earth, were said to be coming from an underground evil, and locals claimed to see fairies dancing around them.

I remember an older woman in that spa who asked another to scrub her back, and how strange it seemed to me, this sort of intimacy between strangers. I, then, was still uncomfortable in my own body, uncomfortable even in a bathing suit; I gave great attention to dressing in oversized clothes, to make sure my jeans did not fit too well, to not show any hint of shape. Even though now I thought of that young body and that I'd happily take her to the grocery store in that bikini. But then again, I wouldn't. Because it was my body now that I would take to the grocery store in a bikini, the one that went with this mind. I remembered Marta asking, playfully but still, if the famous writer had a body.

We only get one body, I'd often say, when urging friends to take care of themselves, not work themselves sick. One capacious body that turns over and over.

Once, a friend, an older writer friend, had said, or maybe he'd written, that women show more and more as the rest of the world wants to see less and less, but he didn't say this with admiration or political intent but a bit of repulsion, and that had always stayed lodged in my mind. At the time I was young, and he didn't seem to equate me with those older women, as though my youth, all youth, were eternal, as though I'd done something special by being young.

Maybe it was Luka who said this, but it was long ago.

The spa had a stand with jewelry, made by a local artist, I recognized the name, and I bought a blue bead on a delicate gold chain and wrapped it around my wrist. It was touristic— the jewelry, not the superstition—yet I felt better.

When I returned, it seemed I had been gone a very long time. I hung the navy-blue dress in the closet.

On the back terrace squatted five empty terra-cotta pots and a few smaller clay ones, filled with herbs, which I watered. The French couple had loved taking care of the garden. I'd added Luka's two plants to the terrace. I would need to repot them soon. Some evenings, a man in a truck drove through the narrow streets with a megaphone, selling those ceramic pots. I'd listen for him.

That night, I opened the balcony doors and stepped outside. The sea was glass, the sea was oil. Everything was still. I slept well until morning.

THE OLD RAILWAY STATION WAS A TWENTY-MINUTE WALK from the house. Although it was no longer in use—the train no longer ran through here—the charming station itself was often visited and photographed. Though not like the river of sand; it was left alone to be captured as it was, as it really was, if that is such a thing at all. As ruins, so photographers might proclaim them beautiful. And though it was never overrun with tourists, a few curious visitors often poked about. The extra switch lines had abandoned coal cars and box freights, and there was also an antique steam engine, proud and gleaming, like an installation. Practical corrugated tin had replaced the roof's red ceramic tiles. In the distance, the mountains echo.

There was a small café and I sat down to have a coffee and closed my eyes, let the morning glow wash over my face. The mist had burned away and the day felt clear and bright.

HERE IN THIS OLD HOUSE, I STILL SOMETIMES WAKE TO the sound of a train, whose call deep in the night couples with images of sandy shores that turn into rock and rocky shores that shift into sand. The call of a train merges into a ferry's horn that merges into the trilling call of an owl, then the song of a nightingale. And then silence. A story slicing through concentric rings. A woman flinging open a door; another standing at the edge of the sea, as if wanting it to absorb her completely. A melody I can almost recognize, a blur of language and space, then a melody I sing. Ancient olive trees and hillsides dotted with houses; hidden caves and craggy black pines and rivers that carve the earth and flow into the sea. The echoey splash of a morning swimmer and a beach with two grand tamarisk trees. Ferries and catamarans and faces I cannot quite recognize, works in translation in which I am still also there, a shadow inside the page.

I am still all those archipelagoes in the distance and that elusive border between land and sea, where I go now, where I go again, where I write myself and erase myself, where I remember myself, again.

Notes

WHEN THE NARRATOR NOTES OTHER WRITERS DIRECTLY, they are attributed in the text. Other times, the narrator echoes them, without direct attribution. These are as follows: The narrator references Susan Sontag, from the essay "Where the Stress Falls," both "To remember is to voice—to cast memories into language—and is, always, a form of address" and the title itself. "Find a beginning" and the rest of the lines from *The Odyssey* are from Emily Wilson's illuminating translation. From book 10, lines 500–511: "The North Wind's breath / will blow the ship. When you have crossed the stream / of Ocean, you will reach the shore, where willows / let fall their dying fruit, and towering poplars / grow in the forest of Persephone." From book 13, line 200: "Where am I now?" From book 5, lines 343–44: "Strip off your clothes and leave the raft behind / for winds to take away." From book 12, line 185: "Now stop your ship and listen to our voices."

The phrase "more-than-human" comes from *The Spell of the Sensuous: Perception and Language in the More-Than-Human World* by David Abram, a writer who has helped shape my perspective. The narrator begins each section with the words of others. They are as follows: Etel Adnan, *Shifting the Silence*; Anne Carson, "Decreation: How Women Like Sappho, Marguerite Porete, and Simone Weil Tell God"; Eleni Vakalo, translated by Karen Emmerich, "The Forest" in *Before Lyricism*; Mary Ruefle, "Pause," in *My Private Property*; and Olivia Laing, *To the River*.

Ideas about translation were formed by my own ongoing attempts at translation from Modern Greek to English, and I'm grateful to wonderful works about the art of translation, such as those by Karen Emmerich (*Literary Translation and the Making of Originals*), Jhumpa Lahiri (*Translating Myself and Others*), and Kate Briggs (*This Little Art*). Karen Emmerich's translation of Eleni Vakalo's *Before Lyricism* greatly inspired this book, including the question the narrator utters about what it means to name things truly. The linguist the narrator cites regarding indirectness and subtext is Deborah Tannen ("Indirectness in Discourse: Ethnicity as Conversational Style"), and she also mentions Salman Rushdie's memoir, *Knife*, and his "palaces" "built out of alphabets" ("I saw majestic palaces and other grand edifices that were all built out of alphabets"). The novel where the Brazilian writer disappears into a tree with a cigar is Idra Novey's *Ways to Disappear*.

The poems the narrator mentions by Nikos Engonopoulos and Manolis Anagnostakis are "Poetry 1948," translated by Kimon Friar, and "To Nikos E.," translated by Karen Emmerich. The narrator alludes to the poem "Maria Nephele" by Odysseus Elytis when she writes and erases her name in the sand. The Albanian novelist who writes about borders is Gazmend Kapllani in his novel *A Short Border Handbook*. The Ottoman travel writer Evliya Çelebi wrote of the hammam of Kyparissia.

The lines "Where had they all gone, these people who had seemed so real?" and "In the dark, the cigarette glowed, like a fire lit by a survivor. But who would see this light, this small dot among the infinite stars?" are from Louise Glück, "A Work of Fiction."

"Tomatoes are redder by the sea" is from Predrag Matvejević, *Mediterranean: A Cultural Landscape*.

A portion of this novel previously appeared, in different form, as a short story entitled "Archipelago" in *Ploughshares*, and descriptions of the narrator's house also appear in a short story called "Kaleidoscope" published in *MQR*.

Acknowledgments

I WOULD LIKE TO EXPRESS MY DEEP APPRECIATION TO MY wonderful editor, Masie Cochran, and also to Becky Kraemer, Isabel Lemus Kristensen, Nanci McCloskey, Jacqui Reiko Teruya, and the rest of the fantastic team at Tin House for their warmth, incisive editing, and attention. Thank you to Beth Steidle for the wonderful artwork and design. I'm grateful to Audrey Crooks for her incisiveness and intelligence and for believing in this book and my work.

I am especially grateful to the support offered by the Murray E. Jackson Creative Scholar Award and the Career Development Chair Award at Wayne State University, the time and and resources provided by which allowed me to dedicate focus and energy to this work. Thank you to my colleagues at Wayne State University, Writing Workshops in Greece, the University of Michigan, and the Warren Wilson College MFA Program for Writers for their intellectual and artistic communities, and to the writers at the Aegean Arts Circle in Andros, Greece.

Though I have attempted in the past to acknowledge all those who have moved me in the making of a book, as I get older I find the undertaking nearly impossible. Where does one begin? To those writers and translators, scholars and artists, whose work inspires and influences me—thank you. I extend a deep gratitude and thanks to all my wonderful friends and family, both near and far, whose support and love, kindness and insight, is invaluable. To my friends with whom I'm in regular joyful conversation, whether across tables or platforms or oceans, and to those old friendships I will always carry inside me—I am grateful to you and for you. "We are a crowd of others," wrote Elena Ferrante, words that prefaced my previous novel but feel all the more true each passing year. And to all the readers: thank you.

I began this book after my father died, and though the story does not address this type of loss directly, living inside grief nonetheless informed the writing. May his memory be eternal. Love and deep gratitude to my brother, Dean, for his wit and warmth, and my mother, Luba, for her love; and most of all to my beloved, Jeremy, with whom I'm grateful, immeasurably, to move through this world.

JEREMIAH CHAMBERLIN

Natalie Bakopoulos is the author of *Scorpionfish* and *The Green Shore*. Her work has appeared in *Ploughshares*, *Ninth Letter*, *Kenyon Review*, *Tin House*, *VQR*, *The Iowa Review*, *The New York Times*, *Granta*, *Glimmer Train*, *Mississippi Review*, *MQR*, *O. Henry Prize Stories*, and various other publications. She received her MFA from the University of Michigan, has received fellowships from the Camargo and MacDowell foundations and the Sozopol Fiction Seminars, and was a 2015 Fulbright Fellow in Athens, Greece. She's an assistant professor at Wayne State University in Detroit. She's on the faculty of Writing Workshops in Greece.